THE LAND
OF THE
PURPLE RING

Also by Deborah J. Natelson

Bargaining Power

Cover by Nada Orlić.
Interior illustrations by Katie Futterwacken.

THE LAND
OF THE
PURPLE RING

Deborah J. Natelson

1

Perpetua

Imagine a land steeped in time.

Not time as we know it, with the swing of pendulums, the ring of alarms, the tick of clocks, the passage of *then* to *now* and back to *then* again and again and again and again. Nor time as a relative factor to be stretched and masticated, organized and sculpted, for time is not chewing gum and ought not be treated as such. Or so the inhabitants of Perpetua would tell you.

Time! You lose time, gain time, look for time, make time, kill time (a violent and wasteful act punishable by up to ten years of clock tower maintenance work), save time, measure time, and otherwise treat time as your most precious commodity. Citizens of Perpetua know this, and they hoard time. They don't have time to be generous or attentive or gracious, but nor do they have time for greed or selfishness or laziness. They don't even have time for time, most of the time.

The Clockmaker, as not only a citizen of Perpetua but a distant relative of Time herself (being the only child of Where Has the Time Gone?), naturally bought into this mentality at quite a reasonable monthly rate. He invested his time into the molding of cogs, the carving of hands and face and fob, the movement and dial. His shop smelled of bronze and oil and glass, and he never had a thought outside of clocks until the Idea came.

IDEA:

A member of the family Imagination (genus Inspiration), the Idea is a small but niggling notion that worms its way unnoticed into a brain. Once there, it hooks itself in and sends out tendrils for nourishment.

An Idea settled is nearly impossible to treat without professional help. In extreme cases, it may resist even the ministrations of Oblivitors, Bleachers, System Restorers, and Brainwashers.

Having no access to professional help, the Clockmaker immediately succumbed to the Idea and got to work. Utilizing his decades of skill, he built a gyroscopic tourbillon of pure diamond. Inside a watch, it would have kept balance no matter which way the watch was turned and maintained a true tick for hundreds of years, but the Clockmaker did not put it inside a watch; he put it on display and called it a heart of crystal: beautiful in the glimmering, glinting, glistening way it inhaled and exhaled light as it spun.

Perpetuans caught the heart's shimmer out of the corners of their eyes and in the warmth of their ticking hearts. Tears gathered and trickled down their cheeks. From the thirteen corners they came—in hordes!—to ooh and ahh and admire and offer hours and years of time in exchange for it.

When word of the wondrous heart whispered in Time's ear, she gathered her troops and marched out to see the source of the fuss.

The people of Perpetua felt the wear and tear of Time's approach and fled from it. They crossed to neighboring cities and hid in cellars full of honey and amaranth and immortelle. They covered their faces and plugged their ears and tried not to breathe, lest she hear them. Time knew they hid and where, and amusement flickered across her bone-white eyes and hard mouth, for none can really hide from the effects of time.

On she marched, the breeze from her passing wearing down the features of stone façades and carving grooves into the abused earth. Stone cracked as she neared, and water evaporated. Flowers sprang up, withered, and died. Every sixty seconds, one of the moles clinging to her jowls sloughed off and fell to the ground. As it landed, it grew—an inch a second until a full-grown minuteman joined the retinue, marching behind his leader in perfect time.

Each minuteman carried a bayonet and wore boots and a blood-red suit, but Time herself wore only the gray of ash on her General's uniform. Even her great leather belt had long faded to gray; and her feet were bare.

So Time crossed Perpetua, her tremendous pace devouring distance until she stood in the threshold of the Clockmaker's humble shop. Day and night, youth and age flashed across her fleshy face, and the wood of the shop rotted, and the clocks within rusted.

The Clockmaker exclaimed as his life's work crumbled before his eyes. "Oh, great Time!" he cried, throwing himself at her flat, bare feet. "I cry you mercy!"

Minutemen stomped their boots and raised their bayonets, but Time only smiled, her face folding in deep, unpleasant creases. She leaned her hand on the doorframe, and it crumbled away. "I have no mercy," she said. "Show me the diamond heart."

The Clockmaker shriveled before her. He was not aging prematurely despite Time's proximity—which itself could bode nothing good. "The heart of crystal is my magnum opus," he said. "It is dearer to me than anything else in the shop, anything else I've ever made. What a waste it would be to destroy it! And yet," he added to himself, "it is so phenomenal that surely even Time could not bear to harm it. Maybe if I show it to her, it will melt her ruthless heart, and she will leave me alive."

Clutching this hope to his chest, the Clockmaker extracted the heart of crystal from its display cabinet and brought it before Time. Its glimmer and shimmer and shine captivated him, as they always did. "Is it not beautiful?" he breathed.

"It's grotesque," Time said. "A heart paraded about without a body? For shame!" She spoke harshly, but the glint of the heart reflected in her milky eyes and sparked desire within her. "Your life is forfeit, Clockmaker, for you have laid eyes upon Time. Yet I can be generous. Build me a mechanical man with this heart of crystal, and I will extend your life a year and a day to complete it."

"A year and a day!" exclaimed the Clockmaker. "But that is not nearly enough time! Even polishing a watch can take me two weeks. Why, a mechanical man would take a lifetime!"

A smirk twisted Time's wide lips. "Then a lifetime you shall have," she said. "You shall live long enough to build me my slave, and not a moment longer. And don't think I won't know if you dither and dally and waste precious seconds!"

This last threat fell upon uncaring ears. The Clockmaker had not before considered making a body for the heart, but Time's words had hooked a new Idea into his brain, and he fell before it.

The Clockmaker's boy came to life at a very young age. Thousands of minuscule cogs whirred and wheeled and ticked away in his clockwork brain. The two independent balance wheels—which had bridges across the hemispheres of his brain and synchronized themselves automatically—were as long as the Clockmaker's thumb; the smallest cogs were so petite that he could see their teeth only under a microscope. Each and every part shone, flawless, under the shop lights.

In those days, the boy had only a heart, a brain, and one ear, so he spent his time feeling and thinking and listening. The Clockmaker spoke to him continually, and so the boy learned what words meant.

"Time may have commissioned you," the Clockmaker told him one day as he labored over a pair of eyes, "and I may build you, but you'll need to be able to repair yourself. I wouldn't trust another clockmaker, if you can avoid it. You never know for whom they might ultimately be working."

"Why do you not trust Time?" asked the boy, much later. His teeth were visible only on the left-hand side, where his jaw had been

skeletonized, and he was still getting used to having a tongue. "I would not exist without her commission—and you would be dead."

"Yes, but neither is any credit to her; she merely wants a slave—one who can withstand her presence. Time has no real appreciation for living beings or art, and you are both."

"But if I am to be a slave," the boy pointed out, "would it not be better if I had neither life nor art? That way, I could not be wasted."

The Clockmaker did not answer immediately. Something by way of revelation was exploding in his brain, and he didn't know what to do about it. He had never had time for family or personal attachments or anything aside from his work.

Only months later, when he had completed four fingers and a thumb and attached digits to hand and hand to arm and arm to torso frame, did he touch upon the topic again.

"It's time for you to learn the craft, my boy," he said. "I've been telling you about it these past three years. How much have you retained?"

"Everything," said the boy.

"Good," said the Clockmaker, and brought over a palm-sized alarm clock. "What would you do with this?"

The boy turned it over in his new hand and examined it with his rather near-sighted eyes. "It looks old," he said. "A family heirloom, maybe. I would remove the rust and polish it up like you polish me."

"That would be beautiful," said the Clockmaker, "but this is where art comes in. The clock is old, and people like old things. We ought to honor its age. So by all means clean up the rust inside and replace any broken teeth, but treat the exterior with respect. Clean it, but do not make it look new."

The boy tilted his head. "But it is tarnished."

"Yes."

"I do not understand," said the boy, "but it does not matter. I do not need to be able to repair clocks, only myself. I am to be a slave, not a clockmaker."

"You are my son," the Clockmaker said firmly, "and I will teach you my profession."

The boy paused, his clockwork brain grappling with this. "I did not know you considered me your son," he said. "I have always considered you my father, of course. Stop! Why are you crying? You will rust."

From that day forth, the Clockmaker taught the boy everything he knew, which was mostly about clocks. In the mornings and afternoons, they worked together on the boy's body, or the Clockmaker worked on the boy while the boy repaired clocks that had been waiting their turn patiently for years. In the evenings, the Clockmaker told the boy stories from his childhood and sang to him in a scratchy voice as they scrubbed the shop free of dust.

The boy's clockwork brain remembered everything it was told, but this knowledge did not automatically transform into practical skill. The Clockmaker had to train him how to hold a broom, scrub brush, and sponge. At first, the boy's fingers were thick and clumsy, but together, he and his father redesigned them until they could eradicate every grain of dirt from the deep corners of the workshop.

Clockmaking required four more revisions of the boy's fingers, considerable brain extensions and fine tuning, and built-in magnifying glasses he could snap over his eyes. His brain itself had to be completely disassembled, cleaned, polished, oiled, and reassembled multiple times during this process, which the boy found vastly disconcerting and which his father found even worse.

The most complicated watches contain over a thousand components, most of them tiny; the boy contained millions, and he learned how to make, assemble, and repair all of them. He could mount anchor crutches between scotch pins, twist springs (whether mainspring, fine-tuning, or spiral torsion), file screw heads, and carve screw threads. Escape wheels did not escape his attention, and his balance wheels spun with the precision of tightrope walkers. He adjusted adjusting pins, slipped tiny weight discs on balance pins to slow fast watches, and shaved weight from balance wheels to quicken slow watches. He mounted, polished, and oiled chatons, and knew the uses and misuses of twelve types of oil. Given a pattern, he could engrave any design.

Yet the Clockmaker remained unsatisfied. "It is not enough

that you can follow instructions," he said. "You must be able to give yourself instructions, invent new designs, and think independently. I will make you a box, but you will have to travel to Imaginarium to fill it."

So the Clockmaker designed a case of pure iron and stored it in the boy's gut. "Inspirations navigate by magnetic fields," he explained, "and are confused by iron. When you escape Time's palace and get to Imaginarium, you'll see for yourself."

In those latter days, the Clockmaker was constantly plotting the boy's escape from Time's palace. He talked about freedom and slavery as he encased visible cogs in metal or glass; he explained about locks and keys as he inscribed his maker's symbol on the boy's collarbone and checked that no screw was too loose or too tight; he emphasized the importance of escaping before Time's presence wore down cogs as he smoothed the boy's kneecaps. "Time," he said, "is of the essence."

After nearly thirteen years of work, the Clockmaker knew he was finally coming to the end. He'd left engraving the boy's nose until last, for this was the one feature he had modeled after his own face. The nose protruded sharply downward and ended in a razor point. The boy could neither smell nor taste, for these things are beyond clockwork, but he would have the most elegantly scroll-engraved nose and tongue imaginable.

"When I finish your left nostril," the Clockmaker said, "you will be complete, my son—and then Time will come for you."

"No, no!" cried the boy. "You cannot be done. I still need—you could polish—" But he was honest, and could think of nothing remaining. "But I do not want to leave you, Father!"

"I have had a good life," said the Clockmaker; "I have gotten to build you. Remember how proud I am of you and all I have told you. And never forget to wind yourself up when you're feeling languid."

"But Father—please!"

"There, there," said the Clockmaker, and three things happened at once: he smoothed the last stroke; he crumpled, dead, to the floor; and Time arrived to collect her property.

The boy had never before traveled past his own front door, and every new sight heralded a new miracle. From his window, he had been able to see the clock tower with its smiling triangle face, and he had supposed that every clock tower had a similar face. Not so. He saw oval faces and round, square and rectangular, heart-shaped and liver-shaped. The clock towers, like every clock they passed, heralded Time's presence by chiming, tolling, booming, singing, or screeching every hour at once.

The boy saw neither people nor animals as they marched, but he saw evidence of far more creativity than he could have guessed existed: sundials, vine-and-ivy clocks, lamppost clocks, hedge clocks, and a great many other things that were not clocks and that, therefore, the boy had not yet learned were to be appreciated.

Not that the boy was in any position to appreciate anything. Quite apart from being surrounded by minutemen, whose stylish caps blocked his view of everything below chin level, he was in a great deal of pain. He thought Time might have damaged something when she'd wrapped her massive mitts around his middle and carried him out of the disintegrating shop, away from the corrugated clocks, crumbling countertops, and most especially away from the figure on the floor sighing into dust. Something certainly *felt* broken. Perhaps she'd cracked the casing of his gyrotourbillon—his diamond heart that kept him ticking away in good balance whether he stood on his hands or on his head or spun at crazy angles.

The boy had never felt anything like this before, and wasn't sure he could diagnose it himself. But he could not ask his father, and who else was there? The minutemen's hands were so thick and clumsy inside their starched white gloves, and Time—

Time had commissioned his existence. It was by her will as it was by the Clockmaker's craft that he had been born, and she should therefore be his mother, as the Clockmaker was his father. And surely *she* would be able to fix him. But when he looked at her marching on, uncaring, he learned what it was to be intimidated, and he stayed silent.

The boy made no attempt to escape. It never occurred to him to try: the Clockmaker had spoken only of escaping Time's palace, not of escaping on the trip there. In any case, such utter wretchedness overwhelmed the boy that he could not have done anything if it *had* occurred to him.

As he sank into this morass of misery, the landscape changed. Gone were the dusty towns, the musty clock towers, and the trusty roads. Present were twenty-six gardens in a great loop, one garden for each hour of the day. They were sunlit or dark, netted with blooms or blooming with nettles, filled with fluttering butterflies or bumping with bats, seasoned with mist or snow or blazing heat.

If the boy had had a sense of smell, he would have swooned; if he had had allergies, he would have sneezed. As it was, his head cleared, and he looked with calm resignation over the coruscating scarlet morning flowers, the toxic midnight toadstools, and the mildly inconveniencing nightshade—to Time's palace.

2

Time's Palace

Her clockwork slave caught unresisting in her wake, Time swept into her palace. That palace would have been the most marvelous museum in the universe, had it been open for exhibition. Nowhere to be found were the classic works. No cross-eyed women peered out from paintings; no naked statues sat contemplatively with chins on fists. No fragments of pottery from long-lost civilizations perched on pedestals, although the civilizations might have, had Time found a way to preserve them behind protective glass.

Ah, but what *was* there! A treasure trove of technology and art lost to the ravages of time! Swords made of Demosthem metal, a type of steel so strong it was said to be able to shear through solid rock. A mechanism that monitored the positions of the stars. The final symphony of the Great Deaf Composer, thought lost when the composer proclaimed he needed to learn the music of the ocean and set out in a dinghy, never to be seen again. Fresh young love dripping endlessly inside a jar, only to reevaporate. The pigment of hair now gray—the health of teeth now rotten—the strength of bones now brittle—sloshing in decanters and sobbing to be lost.

And the art! Many-tentacled sea monsters detailed in arsenic-based acrylics; reliefs depicting the terrible rituals of rubber trolls; garbage statues made of real garbage and smelling of two-week-old salmon. Wreathes of samsonite; a stuffed, snarling saber-toothed tiger; a sculpture radiant with radioactive blood; the tinned lament of the blue chickadee—even the slave's extraordinary perception could not take everything in before he was hurried on and on, through Time's labyrinthine corridors, to the nursery of the O'clocks.

O'CLOCKS:

This family term refers to the thirteen sets of conjoined twins who are Day's offspring: One O'clocks, Two O'clocks, Three O'clocks, Four O'clocks, Five O'clocks, Six O'clocks, Seven O'clocks, Eight O'clocks, Nine O'clocks, Ten O'clocks, Eleven O'clocks, Twelve O'clocks, and Thirteen O'clocks. Each twin embodies either a.m. or p.m. and engorges or deflates according to the time of day.

For example, at midnight, Thirteen O'clock a.m. is bloated round as a ripe grape and Thirteen O'clock p.m. has shriveled raisin-thin. As the clock ticks toward 1 a.m., Thirteen a.m. shrinks while Thirteen p.m. grows. At 6:30 a.m., the twins are of equal size; but the moment the clock ticks 6:31 a.m., Thirteen p.m. has grown larger than her twin. She continues to grow until at noon she is the grape and her sister the raisin.

All of the O'clocks function in this manner, and none has yet complained about what a terribly inconvenient and uncomfortable system it must be.

"I do not know anything about childcare," the clockwork slave said, flipping a magnifying glass over his eyes to get a closer look. It wasn't only their size that altered, he realized, but also their relative ages. Ten O'clock p.m.—the hour at hand—watched him with eyes far more intelligent and comprehending than the slave himself felt at the moment. "How often do they need to be oiled?"

12

"Figure it out," Time replied, and left before he could ask anything further.

The clockwork slave did his best, he really did. He dusted the children every morning and every evening, and made a dehumidifier out of the treasures lining Time's palace so that the children would not rot. There did not seem to be a way to disassemble the children without damaging them, so he poured oil down their intake orifices and rubbed it into their skin. It was not, perhaps, the best oil—he had to make do with what he could find—but he tested it on his own cogs and decided it worked well enough.

The slave shaved the growths from the O'clocks' noggins and polished them with a soft cloth to prevent mold. Much trickier was correcting the children's pendulums. The Clockmaker had always moved very precisely, almost like clockwork himself, and Time marched everywhere. But the O'clocks simply would not cooperate with the slave's attempts to regulate them. He nearly panicked before he remembered that the villagers he'd espied outside the shop window and the boy who had come to deliver the groceries had not moved in proper regimented fashion.

The memory of those groceries bothered him. The Clockmaker had explained to him that eating and sleeping for fleshy beings was like winding up for clockwork. Almost all people, he'd said, whether they were Perpetuans or Grossians or Troils or Forsoothians or any other species, had to eat. The slave had not understood the appeal of food, and had felt rather superior for not consuming it, but now he wondered. He had not found a key to wind up the children, and the children had refused to eat anything he had scrounged for them. They did sleep, however, in between their hours.

In the end, the slave decided to simply keep a close eye on the O'clocks. If he saw any signs of deterioration, he'd ask Time's advice. In the meantime, he'd keep oiling and polishing.

As part of his attempts to get the O'clocks to move properly, and to find food for them, the slave took them on walks around Time's palace. The palace stretched from here to there and back to here again. Even as Perpetuans hoarded time, so Time hoarded space, shoring it up against the knowledge that even she would eventually pass away. Since the slave had never learned how to get lost, he didn't. True, he became what some people might think of as lost. He wandered with the children for days and days (as measured by the O'clocks) without coming back to the nursery; but then, no one had ever told him that he was supposed to stay in one place.

The O'clocks certainly didn't seem to mind. "You're a funny nurseryman," said Seven O'clock a.m., while he waddled along, his twin a sliver against his bulging side. "Why do you pull at your hip whenever my brothers Five are full?"

"I am clockwork," said the slave. "I must wind myself up regularly, or my springs sag and my cogs slow and my tick lags. Only my heart does not need winding, for it is a gyrotourbillon and pure diamond."

Seven contemplated this. "That sounds like a poorly thought-out system," he said. "It's far less sensible than growing and shrinking with the ebb and flow of the day."

"I disagree," said the slave, stung. "Clockwork makes the best sense of anything. While I admire the evenness of your ebb and flow, as you call it, I admire it only because it is as even as clockwork. But fleshy clockwork could never compare to what my father called the beauty of glistening cogs and the precision of the craft."

"Well, what do you know?" said Seven. "You're only a slave. You don't even have a name."

The slave rounded on him. "Of course I have a name!" he cried. "It is 'Boy'!"

He expected this to shut Seven up, and was deeply hurt when instead the O'clock began laughing and laughing, laughing so hard that oil tears oozed from his eyes and his emaciated brother jiggled on his side. "'Boy'!" he screamed with laughter. "You think your name's 'Boy'!"

Something stirred deep in the slave's clockwork brain and thudded in his clockwork heart, sending him momentarily off balance. "Well? It is!"

"You idiot," Seven shouted, in between howls of laughter, "'Boy' isn't a name!"

"It is what my father called me," the slave said stoutly.

"Your father? You mean your maker. I guess he didn't think you were worth enough to give you a real name, not when you were only going to be a slave." Then Seven fell back into paroxysms of laughter that redoubled every time the slave tried to defend himself or his father.

Things being what they were, the slave was quite relieved when Eight O'clock chimed, and Seven had shrunk too young to speak any longer, although he still shook with laughter.

That shaking, the slave reflected, could not be beneficial to proper functioning. Later, when the Sevens were in equilibrium, he'd look to see if their tourbillon needed adjusting.

The hours of each day continued to grow and shrink in proper order. Not one became unsightly either in expanding or diminishing, and no day or minute or season complained. The O'clocks did not precisely flourish under the slave's care, but flourishing was not indicated.

Having demonstrated his competence, the slave's tasks doubled and doubled again and again and again, until he never had a moment of peace. Time herself did not assign him further jobs— indeed, she might have forgotten him, as she was like to forget simple competence without extraordinary feats. Instead, the other occupants of her sprawling palace approached him.

"I sleep during the night," said Day, "but Night is not yet awake to tuck me in."

"I will tuck you in each evening," said the slave.

"It isn't fair," griped Night, when he learned of this arrangement, "that Day gets all the special treatment."

"I am happy to tuck you in each morning," the slave said politely.

"I hear you are taking care of Day and Night and the O'clocks,"

Morning told him, when she heard. "I don't need to be tucked in or to have my nappy changed, but my hair grows at quite an extraordinary rate to keep up with the grass. Won't you trim it for me?"

"Gladly," said the slave, and had collected a room full of hair before the beetle who rolled the Sun toward noon approached him and humbly asked to take it away for his nest.

"We have little ones coming," the beetle explained, rubbing its front legs in shy pleasure. "My wife and I."

"How exciting," said the slave, thinking of the clocks he had built.

"It is," the beetle agreed. "Think of the new star systems! We've agreed to seed them in a beetle constellation. Do you think that's a good idea?"

"Extremely," said the slave, who had built a wristwatch with a miniature constellation on its face. The Clockmaker had told him it was most beautiful and, though the slave did not understand beauty himself, pleasure had welled through him. So he helped the beetle on his way, and then went to repair Time's running shoes and sift the Sands of Time (which the time cats persisted in using as a litter box), and filed birth and death records. He would have liked to repair egg timers and grandfather clocks and even hourglasses, but could find nothing of the sort in Time's palace.

Faster than asparagus cooks, word of the slave's skill and efficiency spread throughout Time's family. Whenever anyone needed child minding or paperwork or things put to order, someone told a scuttling second hand, and the second hand ran to the slave on five fingers and signed to him to follow. No ordinary man could have kept track of the fifteen or forty-three or two hundred seventy-two tasks the slave dealt with simultaneously, but the slave never forgot or neglected a one.

Until he lost the Thirteen O'clocks.

16

He didn't realize at first that he *had* lost the Thirteens. If he hadn't been in the habit of occasionally returning them to their nursery and counting them, he might not have realized his mistake for far longer. As it was, he counted from One to Twelve and then counted again. He searched the nursery and looked into the hallway. He retraced his steps, checking under museum pieces and asking everyone he met, but no one had seen the missing twins and no one was inclined to help him look. They were working, and they were terribly busy. What was the slave for anyway?

The Thirteens were not in the nursery segment, which included artifacts that Time had stolen between 703 and 704.5 years ago. The Thirteens were not a century earlier, where the slave had stopped to repair the ancient tea-time fishing rod; nor were they in the mouse traps that the time cats set. Old Man Time had no memory of seeing any of the O'clocks, though the slave was certain the children had swarmed about his feet as he had told them a long story of days to come. So the slave retraced his steps further, to where he had delivered Gloaming's letter to Twilight—

No. He had first delivered Twilight's letter to Gloaming—

Hadn't he? Or had there been a third party? Tierce, maybe, or—

Or—

He couldn't remember.

Why couldn't he remember? He remembered everything.

The slave slowed and then stopped as a film of horror settled over him. He hunted through his mind for other spots of corroded memory, and the more he checked, the more appalled he became. Now, he could see that he had been slowing down, malfunctioning in small ways, his movements jerkier, his thoughts scattered.

The slave ran to find a mirror. He stood before it and began opening his casing to see what lay beneath.

Rust edged his polished interior, spotting the shiny pieces with orange flecks. Dust and sand collected in nooks, and a spider had made its home behind his heart. One bridge had splintered and another had snapped. Wheels grinned cracked teeth at him. Even the Clockmaker's signature on his collarbone had been worn to near-invisibility under the constant groping of O'clock fingers down the decades.

The slave had no tear ducts, and so could not cry. But if he could have cried, he would have then, for he had disobeyed his father's dying wish.

"I am a living being and I am art," he said, "and I have squandered both."

It was time, past time, that he escaped.

Once he had made his decision, the clockwork man—no longer a slave—moved with his usual efficiency. He did not continue looking for the Thirteens, for now he realized they were truly lost and therefore must have gone where all lost things go—to the Land of the Purple Ring. Nor did he attempt to complete any of his unending tasks before departure; nor did he return to the nursery for a maudlin farewell. He had no belongings to gather, and he knew any repairs he attempted would be undone as he worked or would leave him distracted while other parts of him fell apart or—worst of all—would attract Time's notice.

So he turned sharply and swung one leg after the other, faster and faster until he blurred. After years of exploring, he knew everyone and everything there was to know about Time's palace, and so he did not falter or answer questions or slow until he had reached its deepest roots. There, the elegant apartments had long since degraded into cobwebs and rubble. None of the respectable residents would go down this far, for no one who was anyone lived here, and why would you bother to see someone who was not someone? Besides, everyone down here was as mean as his surroundings, and mostly much uglier.

The clockwork man stopped in front of one hovel, no better or worse than its neighbors, and knocked. "In No Time At All?" he asked politely.

"I'm over here," a voice wheezed.

The clockwork man peered around the broken brick wall to see the potbellied old kettle on the other side.

In No Time At All sneered at him. "Oh, it's you. Did that cursèd general Time send you? Because I'm not interested."

"No, sir. I came on my own. I need your help."

In No Time At All snorted. "You're Time's slave. Help yourself—or have her help you."

"With respect, sir," said the clockwork man, "you bitterly hate Time and consider her your enemy. I am enslaved, and Time's presence is killing me as it killed my father before me. It will do her no service if you help me escape."

In No Time At All's face, deep with the lines of resentment, broke into a shards-of-metal grin. "Thwart Time? Deprive her of one of her favorite slaves?" he cried. He swung his potbelly open for the clockwork man, who scrambled in. "Where would you like to go?"

3
The Antechamber

In no time at all, the clockwork man arrived not in Imaginarium, but in the antechamber thereto—which, he was assured, was the closest option. He tried to thank his savior, but the old fellow was too busy holding his waggling potbelly and chuckling to do more than wave him off and disappear in a puff of steam.

The clockwork man watched him go, and then turned his attention to his surroundings. He had not known countries could have antechambers, but maybe Imaginarium was anomalous in that regard—or maybe Perpetua, antechamber-less, had been the anomaly. But how did one move from antechamber to Imaginarium? He must not delay, not again. He'd fall the rest of the way apart!

Or would he? It was immediately clear to the clockwork man that time flowed differently here. In the palace, corrosive time had worn at everything as surely as sandpaper wears at balsa wood; in Perpetua, time was perpetually, perceptibly present—not gentle and distant, as it was here. The clockwork man felt much as a rock climber who has ascended from sea level to ten thousand feet feels: dizzy, nauseous, and disoriented. It was therefore unsteadily and confusedly that he began to walk and take stock.

The Antechamber boasted between two and twenty thousand marvel-makers, depending on the season, and included everything imaginable—not imaginable by you or by me, but by anyone anywhere anywhen. Ideas, Notions, Obsessions, and other particles frequently leaked into the Antechamber and infected the people there. So the inventors and artists and musicians and writers and architects came to be infected, and the clever businesspeople followed them in and set up shop.

Thousands of institutions sprouted up to support the infected folk. General shops offered supplies (drafting paper? Fabric? Hydrochloric acid?). Hot balloon stores sent up customers wanting to try new parachute designs (payment up front, please); smithies rented space to hopefuls; singing instructors wandered the musical aisles, and singing agents trailed them. A runway bisected the Antechamber, broad enough for four plane-like structures to take off side by side. The clockwork man watched the flying contraptions briefly, but was far more interested in the bridge crossing over the runway; he took the free tram back and forth seven times to examine the mechanics, and then once more to end up on the opposite side.

In addition to suppliers, the clockwork man passed many establishments catering to the basic necessities of fleshy beings, from food and drink to sleep and clothing. The clockwork man mostly ignored these, since he had no personal use for them, but he did hear a number of things that confused him—or, rather, a number of numbers. For although he was fairly certain that time was not tangible enough around here to barter, customers nevertheless traded numbers for services. In this way, he learned that a massage cost 43, a soda 1.5, and shoes anywhere between 12 and 210—but he didn't learn 43, 1.5, 12, or 210 *what*.

In No Time At All had dropped the clockwork man off in the Invention District, and the man didn't realize there were different districts until a sign accosted him: "Art District!" the sign screamed in the clockwork man's face. "You're entering the Art District!"

The Art District! Finally, the clockwork man had found what he sought; for surely, here was his path to Imaginarium—and to understanding what art was. His heart spun with excitement. "I am a living being, and I am art," he said to himself—and wondered if there were perhaps others like him here.

21

The Art District, he soon found, was compact to the Invention District's expanse. Storefronts lined one side of each street, plastered with artwork; on the other side, the artists themselves sat or stood or snoozed by easels and under tarps and next to gutters. This was, of course, an artist's natural environment, although the clockwork man didn't realize it at the time. Nor did he realize that if the artists rusted, which fleshy beings seldom did, they would only consider it an extension of their artistic masterpieces.

The basic types of store in the Art District didn't vary much from those in the other districts, but their contents certainly did. Only in the segment devoted to performance artists and lunatics could one find as wide a variety as was commonplace among the inventors. Chisels were mainly found among the sculptors, rubber and wood among the printers, and spiral glass-tipped pens with sparkly ink among the drawers. The painters had stores entirely devoted to canvases, linseed oil, and natural bristle brushes made from 583 different species. Pencils could be found everywhere, as could sketch paper. The clockwork man knew because he examined everything in every shop he passed until one shopkeeper asked him point blank if he had any money, and he said no. After listening to the ensuing diatribe, the clockwork man decided that shops were probably a waste of time anyway, and decided to educate himself via the art rather than the dealers.

When this occurred, he happened to be in a painting section— primarily representational paintings done in oils, although there were abstract paintings mixed in. He went up to each painting in turn and stared at it, taking in the brush strokes and fingermarks, observing the mix of colors, and reading the captions.

Those captions interested him particularly, because they made sometimes far more sense to him than their paintings and sometimes far less. A rose in a jar was usually titled "Rose in Jar," but it was sometimes titled "Constricted Love." The more thoughtful artists had provided explanations for their obtuse titles.

In this way, the clockwork man learned. He did not always understand everything, but he gathered that paintings and captions conformed to patterns—that certain colors were used together more often than not; that when colors met they could blur; and that titles tended to be brief and certainly no more than one sentence long.

Then he came across a caption that broke the pattern. Its painting was a dramatic night scene with a red plant slashed across it like lipstick. The caption read:

Soaking branches twined together over shrubs of gorse and heather
Can do naught to hide the pleasure of the swollen harvest moon.
Owls hunting, preying, hooting, pause nocturnal life-blood looting,
Hide from brilliant stars that, shooting, warn of what is coming soon,
What will crawl out from the ground and spread its ruby petals—soon.
Witch's bane and witch's boon.

Ah, the cruel lusts are rising, pain and fear and death advising,
Whispering secrets—lies or truth—that color minds in vibrant hate.
Hear it stirring, shifting, waking, roots through dirt and worms a-raking,
Pushing up its head and breaking through the night air, deep and late.
Those who have not fled will flee too slow, too frail, too sad—too late.
They will die, but death is fate.

Blood-red berries thrive by moonlight, thrust their petals into plain sight
That the vengeful come and pluck them, brew them in their vile quest.
Poison one and con another, pry a child from her mother,
Sin their goal; they have no other. Let the victims fall oppressed.
Let the villains' conscience' smite them; guilt and agony oppressed. . . .
Then can at last the plants digest.

23

The clockwork man had no idea what to make of this. He read it over a second time and a third. On his fourth go-over, he was interrupted by a breezy little voice saying, "Ah, hah! Finally, someone who appreciates good poetry!" and a fluvron clapping him on the shoulder.

FLUVRON:

Refugees from the planet Vatavia, the fluvrons were first recorded approximately nine decades ago in the Imaginarium Antechamber.

Naturally deleterious to all water-containing environments, these fluorine-based life forms swiftly adapted by creating first a contract and then a symbiotic relationship with clever glass-a-forms. Each clever glass-a-form gives its fluvron shape and solidity, and each fluvron gives its clever glass-a-form symbiont a cheery yellow tint.

Nowadays, these volatile, electro-negative, highly corrosive beings are in high demand as film critics, fashion designers, and poets. . . .

"Greetings," said this particular fluvron. "I am The World's Greatest Poet—but no doubt you guessed that upon reading my work."

"I am sorry," said the clockwork man. "I am afraid I know nothing of poetry."

"Nothing! Hmm. At least you acknowledge it—unlike some people." The World's Greatest Poet floated around him judgmentally. "You've never written poetry?"

"I had never even heard of it, before you told me what it was," the clockwork man admitted.

"And now that you have, you can't wait to try it yourself!"

The clockwork man didn't know how to answer; he was far too honest to tell the fluvron what he clearly wanted to hear. At length, he said, "I am not sure I understand it. It seems to simply be a way

24

of saying very little at unnecessary length."

The World's Greatest Poet guffawed and swirled out a tentacle to poke at the clockwork man's chest. "You've caught the heart of it, dear sir! The nubbin, the bone, the soul of what will one day make poetry the most popular art form—for there is nothing people love more than to go on and on when everyone else wishes they'd just shut up and give someone else a turn! Well spoke, sir, well spoke!"

"Filling impressionable life forms with your nonsense again?" scathed a second fluvron, sidling up to them with the gentle clink of glass. "I'm The World's Even Better Poet, by the way," he told the clockwork man. "And you are?"

"It is *not* nonsense," snapped the first fluvron. "I've seen the nonsense *you* write. It doesn't even rhyme! It has no meter!"

"Which is what makes it superior. It's the feel of the words that matters, not the cheap tricks one uses."

"Hah! The excuse of laziness!"

"If you do not mind, sirs," said the clockwork man, "I feel I cannot follow this conversation without a demonstration. The World's Even Better Poet, how would you have captioned this painting?"

Both poets seemed to like this. The World's Greatest Poet first read aloud his creation with great energy and aplomb, and did his work justice by enjoying the sound of his own voice exceedingly. Then The World's Even Better Poet, who had been studying the slash of red paint over darkness, struck a pose and proclaimed his caption:

"The ravenous berries
bled."

The World's Greatest Poet waited.

The clockwork man waited.

The World's Greatest Poet said, "That's it?"

The World's Even Better Poet smiled smugly. "Of course, my dear colleague. What you don't understand is that the true art of poetry is saying a very great deal in as few words as possible. Stick with me, dear chap," he told the clockwork man, "and I'll teach you *good* technique."

"Modern trash, you mean," sniped The World's Greatest Poet.

"Is poetry art also?" asked the clockwork man, thoroughly baffled by this point.

"My dear sir," proclaimed The World's Greatest Poet. "It is not just art—it is the pinnacle of art. It is living art."

"Brilliantly said, old chap," said The World's Even Better Poet. "Do you mind terribly if I write that down?"

"Not at all, my dear fellow. Not at all."

The poets retired to a nearby tavern, and the clockwork man accompanied them, listening intently. He observed curiously as the poets downed shot after shot of water until they slumped gently over their tables and fell silent. He continued to wait and observe until it became clear the poets wouldn't be good for anything until sleep wound them back up.

The clockwork man's father had told him firmly, again and again, to beware other clockmakers. The last time the clockwork man hadn't been mindful of his father's words, his mind had begun disintegrating; he was determined to be more careful henceforth. But what was he to do? He needed to repair himself, and no one but clockmakers would have the correct tools. Besides, his heart ached to be surrounded by the eviscerated entrails of sickly clocks; to slot their minuscule cogs back into place; to align their freshly repaired teeth; to spend eight hours engraving half a square inch of steel or bronze, linden or maple. His fingers twitched, and his razor nose pointed his steps. He didn't know the solution, but he had always been taught that with patience and hard work, any wheel could be polished to a mirror shine.

Just as the night's cold lights flashed into the brilliant warmth of morning, the clockwork man arrived in the Alley of Clockmakers.

What he found there was not what he had seen in his father's shop, for his father had only had two Ideas in his life, and his work in general was brilliantly executed but not more than ordinarily imaginative. Here, every building—for clockmakers could not work in the open without risking damage or loss—hosted a unique collection. One shop housed a display of terribly naughty clocks. Instead of ticks, these clocks shouted insults at passersby and celebrated the quarter hours with increasingly unprintable words. The cuckoo versions had boys pulling girls' hair and girls slapping boys, men tying cans on cats' tails, and women chopping up their husbands along with the firewood. Another shop specialized in perversions of nature: snake heads on bird bodies, printer cartridges in typewriters, and blatant anachronisms in history texts carved into toe moldings and overlays. One workshop created its clocks inside-out, so that wheels exploded outward to hide shy faces. The clockwork man saw clocks with two faces or ten, with multiple independent sets of gears or gears set floating inside glass spheres. He saw sun-powered clocks and son-powered clocks; clocks powered by the sea and clocks powered by being seen; plushy clocks and pimply clocks and pompous clocks. The older clocks naturally had 13 hours or 26, but already the Antechamberians were adapting to the 24-hour day.

Guilt lanced through the clockwork man's heart at this, but what could he do? The Thirteen O'clocks were in the Land of the Purple Ring now.

At the end of the alley, where it merged with the lamellaphone corner of the musical quarter, the clockwork man came across a display that puzzled him greatly. It must be a clock shop, he supposed, because he could see the paraphernalia of clock making neatly organized on the worktable and could make out the labels on some of the drawers. He saw tubes for inserting suspension wires, hand pullers, a variety of wrenches and nuts, balance support blocks, poising tools, punches for every type of wheel, and clamps. Reamers, cutters, and adapters made his hands twitch. His eyes caught on whale blubber, kerosene, polyalphaolefins and esterns, spindle and citronella, and half a dozen other oils he had never even heard of but which he yearned to experiment with.

All these things, he saw from the window or in person, when he picked the lock and let himself in. All these things—but not a solitary minute hand anywhere; not a second hand or hour hand or face. Not even a moon dial. Instead, the clockwork man found a collection of elegant boxes, many of them not much larger than matchboxes. He picked up one of these and wound it. It didn't wind far, and when he released the crank, the box began chiming the hour.

This struck the clockwork man as terribly wrong; it wouldn't be 7 a.m. for another 29 minutes, 14 seconds.

You see, he didn't understand about music boxes.

MUSIC BOX:

Since the day the famous Omnivarian poet and play-wright W.S. Jostlepike's words "if music is the food of lunch, sing on" brought edible music to the popular view, musical eateries have popped up in many forms. Such delicacies vary widely in quality, of course. The humble Boom Box Bistro—where tinny renditions of popular songs come in paper boxes—is hardly on par with the decadent Restaurant d'Musique—where only the finest sonatas are served on glass plates.

Most popular, however, is the music box café. For a very reasonable fee, customers can rent a music box at the counter to crank at their tables.

Increased demand for original music and music box designs has, inevitably, sparked increased interest in the music and clockwork industries. . . .

"Who are you?" asked a sharp voice.

The clockwork man turned and considered the speaker cautiously. The angle of her nose echoed his own, and the twist of her spine reminded him achingly of his father. "You are a Perpetuan," he observed to her. "Why do you make clocks without faces?"

"How else can I spite Time?" the woman asked.

The clockwork man shook his head.

"Not everything made of clockwork is a clock," she said. Her voice softened from its point, and she stepped forward, raising her hand to stroke his skeletonized cheek, touch the worn maker's symbol on his collarbone. "What are you? I have never *seen* such fine work."

"You are not a clockmaker?" the clockwork man clarified. "What are these, then?"

"Music boxes. Listen." She took the box from his hand, wound it, and released. Tinkles of sound sparkled and twinkled out like a stream in full sunlight.

The clockwork man listened carefully, thinking that this must be music as opposed to just sound, and memorizing it for later comparison. "I have a deal to offer you," he said.

Over the following days and weeks and months, the clockwork man went to meet the poets whenever the lights darkened. No celestial beings lit the Antechamber by day or night, because the Antechamber had no sky, and all the famous thespians stayed on the ground. Instead, day and night were determined by the brightness of the business lights; and, by regulation, these were a dim, purplish blue beginning at 10 p.m.—a change that prompted the hibernating lampposts to exude their own glow. The next morning, at 6 a.m., switches would flick, and the Antechamber would abruptly and brilliantly light up in gold.

The poets were more than happy to fulfill their promises to teach the clockwork man good poetry. The World's Greatest Poet taught him the difference between odes and elegies; villanelles, terza rimas, and terzanelles; epigrams and epics; haiku and blank verse (hideous poems without rhymes!); and, most especially, the pinnacle of poetic form, the most magnificent, romantic, and best style—the sonnet.

"But what makes it the best?" the clockwork man wanted to know.

The World's Greatest Poet started in astonishment. "Isn't it obvious? What could be more lovely, more elegant than twelve lines of quatrains followed by a volta-infused couplet? What meter more flawless than iambic pentameter?"

"Are there no other poems that use quatrains and couplets and iambic pentameter?"

"Ah, but beauty is more than that," explained the fluvron. "Think of the greats—Edmundus Suspenders, Wilhelm Worthwords, Johann Keets. No? What of W.S. Jostlepike? You *must* have heard of him—

> "... pop is not pop
> That flattens when it oscillation finds."

"I did mention," the clockwork man humbly reminded The World's Greatest Poet, "that I was completely unfamiliar with poetry before meeting you."

"I know that," The World's Greatest Poet said, "but I could hardly believe—! Well, young man, listen to a few of these."

The clockwork man did listen, and not to just a few—over the following weeks, he memorized every poem The World's Greatest Poet could recite. And, indeed, he learned everything The World's Greatest Poet could teach him. Soon, he could buy shoes for iamb feet, waltz with trochee or with paeans, dance through the dark in the depths of a dactyl, sing spondees, and greet great green molossi. The amphibrach called to him ... but he could not call back; for while the clockwork man could recite whatever he heard, define the metrical foot of any word, and list rhymes, he could not create a new poem of his own.

"You're constricting him with your rules and regulations," sneered The World's Even Better Poet. "You're enslaving him to the cruelty of meter and rhyme, when what he needs is to be set free."

"Oh, not this again," groaned The World's Greatest Poet. "Indolence!"

"You have taught him your style," said The World's Even Better Poet. "It's time to teach him mine."

And thus the clockwork man spent the hours of night learning, all the while watching the poets drinking shot after shot of water until their stomachs bubbled with hydrofluoric acid and they stumbled home for the night. When the poets retired early, the clockwork man paced the Antechamber, questioning the inhabitants on their imagination-driven works or simply looking and learning.

Without fail, he arrived back at the music box shack at the shattering of day and began work on whatever the music box maker had left out for him the night before. She always joined him within an hour, fresh and bright eyed, to work on other projects or to watch and admire his work.

"Where did you learn to polish like that?" she might ask.

"From my father," he would say. "The Clockmaker."

"Clearly, you're a clockmaker too."

The clockwork man kept his head down and worked on.

"Can your father not help you repair yourself?"

"No," said the clockwork man, "for my father is beyond repair. Time killed him." His hands and voice malfunctioned slightly as he said this, and he steadied them firmly. Precision work did not allow for trembles.

"I have a name, you know," the woman said at one point. "It's Vialia."

"Oh," said the clockwork man. And, because more was clearly indicated, he added, "That is useful to know."

At noon exactly, the clockwork man would stop work on whatever his project was and move into his self-repairs. This was a difficult and delicate duty. First he had to identify the problem areas, and then he had to work methodically and with utmost meticulousness. For those spots in his back and out of view, he set up a system of mirrors and worked back to front and, on one memorable instance, upside down.

Despite his determination to accept no help from anyone even remotely a clockmaker, on several occasions there was work he simply could not do by himself—such as disassembling and reassembling each of his hands in turn and reaching inside his back at the most awkward angle conceivable. He had observed that Vialia's skill level drooped considerably below his own, but she took instruction exactly, and he regretfully supposed that if the wheels inside his back weren't as flawlessly polished as he'd like, at least he'd never have to look at them.

"You know," Vialia told him, after they'd been working together for several months, "you'll always be welcome here."

"I did not know," said the clockwork man, "but I do now."

"You don't have to leave when you've finished your repairs. You could live here with me."

The clockwork man regarded her questioningly. "But I must go to Imaginarium. My father—"

"Your father is dead," said Vialia. "You are alive. You can make your own choices."

"No, I cannot," said the clockwork man; "I have not visited Imaginarium yet."

"Fine, then. Visit. But come back to me after that, and we'll work together. You can create clocks, and I'll create music boxes. Think of how much we could learn from each other! And there are so many other people you can learn from. Your poet friends are only the start."

Vialia had met The World's Greatest Poet and The World's Even Better Poet on dozens of occasions, and because she knew they were his friends, had never once passed judgment on them that the clockwork man could hear. She even invited them to hold some of their sessions in her shop, and at other times she joined them in the tavern to listen and learn. Unlike the clockwork man, her imagination was inbuilt; and under the poets' guidance, she learned to write six types of poem. The clockwork man, who could parse a hundred times more types of poem, could not write a single one.

"I do not know what decisions I will make after I visit Imaginarium," the clockwork man told Vialia, when she continued to insist. "I have never had an imagination before."

Day and night flickered past with their artificial lights. The clockwork man slipped his last cog into place, sanded off the last speck of rust, and applied the last drop of oil.

"Don't forget to come back after you find what you're looking for," Vialia told him, the edge of desperation in her voice. "You'll need to show me what you've learned—and the poets, too."

The clockwork man did not argue. He had had this conversation with Vialia often enough that she knew his answer. He strode in perfect rhythm out of her shop and through the Music District and around Toymaker Junction and up the Grand Staircalator. Vialia trotted behind him, ducking past meandering parades and conga dancers.

At the very top of the Grand Staircalator, The World's Greatest Poet and The World's Even Better Poet waited, up hours before their time.

"We had to say goodbye, old chap," said The World's Even Better Poet.

"And to remind you never to slacken your rhymes or meters," said The World's Greatest Poet.

"And to give you a name," said The World's Even Better Poet, and both fluvrons turned to Vialia. The clockwork man turned too.

Although rather out of breath and panting, Vialia nodded. "Yes," she said. "It's tradition. A father teaches his son his craft and also gives him his name. *You* are the Clockmaker now."

The clockwork man opened his mouth to protest, but the poets beat him to it.

"It's a way of honoring him," said The World's Greatest Poet.

"Of keeping him alive, though he's dead," agreed The World's Even Better Poet.

The clockwork man looked from one to the other to the third, feeling as if the oil in his throat had coagulated. He tried to say "Thank you," but the words wouldn't emerge. So he nodded civilly to the poets and the music box maker before turning to step through the Grand Entrance to Imaginarium.

4
Imaginarium

Imaginarium is the land of imagining happy fluffy clouds, rainbow unicorns, and princesses in towers—but it is also the land of imagining yourself a fluffy cloud who eats rainbow unicorns and locks princesses in towers, for lunatics are no more imaginative than sanetics; no, nor any less. Neither chemical imbalance naturally induced nor chemical stupor knowingly indulged either increases or decreases the base imagination quotient of an individual, though such perversions can impact the presentation of that imagination.

What *can* increase or decrease the imagination quotient is the substance of Imaginarium.

Upon its natal day, back when Time marched around with ash-gray ribbons in her hair, Imaginarium was composed wholly of primordial ooze, petite tufts of weedy islands, thick air, and the Stench.

What a Stench. More suffocating than water, more viscid than ice, more pervading than steam, this was not a stench that stole quietly up to tap you on the shoulder and humbly beg bus fare. This Stench tackled you, pummeled you, and made off with not only your wallet but also the boots from your feet, the fillings from your teeth, the hair from your head, and the breath from your lungs. It left your life intact, however, and repaid you for the mugging by coating your feet and teeth and head and lungs with such inspirations as could make a dragon turn from gold lust to creation must.

Even as the primordial Imaginarium changed its invaders, so the invaders changed Imaginarium a few boots at a time until it became what it was at the Clockmaker's entrance—a place no less perilous than in its youth, but with perils so varied that none could predict them. Indeed, such ubiquitous fickleness of peril rendered warning useless. That was perhaps why no one had bothered to mention to the Clockmaker that a stroll through Imaginarium's garden was no walk in the park; that the breezes weren't a breeze when the Stench was around; that pieces of cake were never easy as pie; and that if you could do it with your eyes shut, it was probably only because opening them would cause blindness, madness, and vertigo—in that order.

The Clockmaker, heart swelling in the glorious awareness of finally fulfilling his father's counsel, extended one clockwork leg and pushed through the threshold and into knee-deep sludge.

The sludge farted as he sank, and the memory of Stench swarmed the Clockmaker's nose, searching for nostrils that did not exist and then, in increasing desperation, experimenting with entering other orifices. But it found only gleaming gears and springs and a pleasant orchestral rendition of tick-tock. Finally, it despaired of him and settled back down to await its next customer.

The Clockmaker observed his sunken limb with displeasure. True, he was waterproof to thirty fathoms—but also true that there was no waterproofing dignity.

Bowing to the inevitable, the Clockmaker squelched, pbbbted, buped, and fwipped through the sucking mud toward the bank. He looked around all the while, in search of a suitable subspecies of Imagination to trap in his iron box and stuff into his gut. Only as he looked did he realize that he did not know what an Idea, Notion, Conviction, Conception, or other species of Imagination looked like, or whether any old piece of Imaginarium would do.

The glomping mud bubbled and muttered for only a short distance in each direction. Had the capricious threshold deposited him only twelve paces to his three o'clock or twenty-six to his eleven o'clock, he would have landed in a field of hydrangeas or in a pit without any bottom but with plenty of noses and mouths and needle teeth spun from sugar. At six o'clock stretched an apparently barren wasteland, and at eight a mountain range of what might have been snow or ice cream or mashed potatoes; the Clockmaker stood too far away to see, and anyway, it might have changed before he arrived. Quite to his disappointment, nothing in view resembled clockwork, metal, or anyone to explain the rules of the place.

The Clockmaker slooped out of the mud and into the field of hydrangeas. He crushed and dirtied a swath ten feet in, and then sat down, plucked a handful of flowers, and began smearing his mucky shins and feet clean. The mud came off readily, but he continued plucking hydrangea pompoms and polishing down to the tiniest detail. He worked with such habitual diligence that he did not realize the curious occurrences in his clockwork brain until he was lost in them.

That caption that The World's Greatest Poet had added to the berry painting . . . the Clockmaker found he approved wholeheartedly of the rhyme and meter. They worked perfectly for a dark and morbid poem. Only . . . only, wouldn't the melancholy menace of its tone have been more appropriately applied to an avian subject? Why this might be the case, he could not say; he was too unused to abstract thinking to effectively dissect it.

The truth was, of course, that the Clockmaker had just had his first Intimation. As far as the Imagination family went, it wasn't much (as a subspecies of the Hint in the genus Hypothesis, Intimations ranked barely above Inklings). Still, we must all begin somewhere, and the Clockmaker took to it like Brussels sprouts to butter. He grabbed another lavender pompom and rubbed it on his skin, massaged it in his hands, crushed it on his head, and generally experimented on the best way to extract the imagination from it.

It didn't take the Clockmaker long to determine that lavender hydrangeas only gave Intimations, whereas pink gave Inklings and blue gave Suspicions. If he'd known more (or, indeed, anything) of horticulture, he might have determined that this was because pink grew in the most basic soil and blue in the most acidic. As it was, he could only experiment, gorging himself on Hints until hardly a flower remained.

The Clockmaker plucked out the central blooms from the last hydrangea of each color and placed them in his iron gut box. Then he moved on. He had inklings and suspicions and intimations that hydrangeas were the least of what Imaginarium had to offer.

The Clockmaker had long ago passed the chasm of sugar-spun teeth, and the mashed-potato mountain had been discovered and eaten while he wasn't looking. Here and there muttered mud pots, but nothing else struck him as familiar, so he kept going in a straight line until he reached a vast boneyard.

At that time, the Clockmaker had not yet learned that people felt uncomfortable and creeped out by the dead. As he had no qualms with taking apart, refurbishing, and replacing his own limbs, he looked upon the boneyard with the cool eyes of a tyro painter gazing upon a collection of natural bristle brushes from 583 different species.

Crushing the flowers had been adequate to release their Hints, but the Clockmaker soon found this technique insufficient for bones, for when he shattered them, their dust flew everywhere and blinded him while their contents escaped. Bones required special technique. After some experimentation, he found that he could crack them gently and peel them like eggshells. The imagination lay within, to be slurped out—only, since the Clockmaker could not slurp, he smeared the marrow over his casing, and thus extrapolated their contents.

Extrapolations, whether Calculations, Estimations, Prognostications, Computations, or Ratiocinations, did nothing to flood the Clockmaker's mind with new information. Instead, they used existing information in combination. He began putting together meaning from disparate elements: the exchange of coins that accompanied the purchases and numbers; the way that the arguments and seeming animosity between The World's Greatest Poet and The World's Even Better Poet did not stop them from spending their evenings in cheerful comradery; the difference between his experiences of friendship and what he had seen of his father's life, which had been solitary before his boy's birth—and what his father's might have become, if he had survived his son's departure.

Days rolled into weeks as the Clockmaker toiled grimly through the boneyard. He remembered every Extrapolation he opened, though they evaporated soon enough. When he reached the end of the boneyard, he stored five types of marrow in his iron box. But though he had begun to learn, he was far from understanding what his Extrapolations meant as he left the razed boneyard behind and entered the linen closet of Empathy.

Behind the Clockmaker, an anomalous alteration overtook the flower field. Whereas before the hydrangeas had grown like perfectly ordinary plants, their colors reflecting nothing more extraordinary than whether people had dropped coffee grounds or woodchips upon their soil, the new flowers grew irregularly. Some appeared almost ordinary, save for an elegant streak of brass or steel or gold along their petals, reflecting dimly in Imaginarium's pervasive twilight. Others grew on rigid steel spines that bent into trellises for their neighbors to twine and climb. Some flowers resembled cogs that meshed with their neighbors and spun in the breeze as Stench rushed by. They did not tell time, but their relation to clockwork was otherwise unavoidable— first cousins at most. Beneath them, roots ticked as they inched and centimetered through the soil, and leaves twitched in sharp, precise flutters.

Most telling, however, if not of time, was the bush at the field's center. Every flower on it grew translucent as diamond and swung on its stem as if on a triple axis. And if a traveler stopped close by and listened very carefully, he would be able to hear the breeze whistling love through the field's heart of crystal, and rejoice with the plant in its life and beauty.

When the Clockmaker had first begun his quest in Imaginarium, it had been out of filial love and duty. The longer he stayed, however, the more he forgot his true purpose in his desperation for *more*—for the more he learned, the more he realized the depths of his ignorance and limitedness. No sooner had he tasted Perception than he craved Detail. Self-Awareness took him up and tossed him into the cosmetic valley of Despair, where he wallowed in foundation and rouge. Fortunately for him, no land of Despair can protect its borders from Hope, which slides in on the molecules of air and is even more pervasive than the Stench.

Hope led him to Perspective, which, although miserable, did not threaten to drown him. The Clockmaker teetered about on its seesaws for ages until they tipped him gently into Creation's bakery.

There, the Clockmaker found himself quite at home, for he perceived that he could extrapolate the designs he had learned from his father and seen in Time's palace and the Antechamber to create his own designs. He marched methodically across the bakery, crumbling pastries to extract their gooey centers and reveling in the distinctions between raspberry and snozzini, sour and sweet, bitter and spicy, paprika-ish and bland. He learned everything a lemon tart could impart and the buttery divisions of a croissant.

With his new understanding, the Clockmaker found himself discontent with the Designs of danishes and the Beauties of butteries and the Intricacies of icing. Why should he recreate these as they were and as others had created them before? So he peeled apart sheets of phyllo and combined them with pie filling, mixed poppy seeds with cranberries and custard, and substituted banana for coconut oil and plantain for banana and coconut chips for plantain and coconut oil for coconut chips—and roasted his concoction in marsh gas.

When the Clockmaker had taken all that Creation's bakery had to offer, he ran into real difficulty, for he found his iron box was full. He kneaded and crushed the ingredients, but he had kneaded and crushed them so often before that he could squeeze out only the last molecules of air and replace them with nothing more than a single poppy seed.

After some contemplation, the Clockmaker told himself, "I do not have to discover a solution now, for here in Imaginarium, my creations will stay as I created them. Only if I leave must they be imprisoned in iron. But how am I ever to leave? And why should I want to leave?"—for he had not yet learned about Adventure.

Inspiration struck the Clockmaker with a brick the moment he stepped into its construction zone. He was fortunate—only a small Idea had hit him—but even so, he remained sprawled for several minutes gingerly feeling his head. The urge to spin auroch hair into toeless socks enveloped him. "What a marvelous idea!" he said—for all Ideas seem marvelous in their initial concussions.

The Clockmaker stood back up and, wary of danger, caught a falling anvil with his arms instead of his head.

"What an even more marvelous idea!" he exclaimed. "Here is plenty of iron with which to build myself a bigger box!" He immediately looked around and found the Forge of Forging Ideas and the Hammer of Hammering Out Ideas and the hot air billows of Excessive Expectations and got to work. Using his experience molding metal and extrapolating creations, the Clockmaker soon made himself a new box, ten times the size of the old one. Naturally, it was far too large to install in his gut, but he could carry it along in his arms without undue difficulty.

"But what if this is not big enough?" he asked himself, looking at it. "It is much larger, but Imaginarium might be too large for it. What if I cannot fit everything I want in here?"

He hunted until he found an iron vein that his surveys indicated stretched down miles and miles into Imaginarium.

"I will make a wheelbarrow," he decided, "and drag it along behind me." But no sooner had he found a brain pick and carved out enough iron for a wheelbarrow than a clockwork carriage occurred to him—or perhaps a train to which he could add endless carriages, that he might never run out of space. Indeed, there seemed no reason he should ever stop expanding.

The Clockmaker worked harder and harder, swinging the pick carelessly and barely getting out of the way of flying Notions. At first, he unearthed mounds of iron, but then it seemed to him that the quality of iron was lessening—and if there was one thing his father had taught him, it was to never use inferior materials. So he worked even harder and more desperately, hunting for the quality iron he had been *so sure* lay beneath him. Yet the more deeply he delved and the more aggressively he attacked, the less iron he found, until he was digging in plain dirt.

What in Imaginarium could be going on? The Clockmaker straightened and looked around. It had been many weeks since he had last bothered, and he had to check his memory to make sure it wasn't faulty—for instead of Ideas and Notions flying wildly about, only a few wispy boxes floated by. He snatched at one, and found he held nothing but the fool's gold of Writer's Block. Worse yet, all the iron he had dug out had evaporated, save for the iron box he had made out of that first anvil Idea.

The Clockmaker fell upon his face, groaning. Months had passed since he had last thought to polish himself. His oil had gone clumpy; his skin was dinged and dented and scraped; and his ticks echoed hollowly. His friends in the Antechamber would not have known their gleaming, meticulous clockwork man, and the Clockmaker could not bring himself to recognize, let alone ameliorate, the situation.

Little did he realize it then, but the fault of this lay in his own greed. For when he had pushed out the last molecule of air from his gut, he had also pushed out the last molecule of Hope. Since then, the foundation of Despair had oozed through all his crushed Hypotheses and Extrapolations and Self-Awarenesses, suffocating them and turning them to its own purpose.

It was in this attitude—prostrate with despair in the Wasteland of Writer's Block—that Vamazz the Vamazing found him.

VAMAZING:

Scholars diverge over the probable etymology of this portmanteau. The majority claim it to be the inevita-

41

ble combination of "very" and "amazing." However, a small but vocal minority insists it instead derives from "verily amazing"—which is to say, amazing in fact and actuality rather than merely in perception or colloquialism. An even smaller and more vocal minority provides compelling evidence that the term was coined specifically in reference to Vamazz and should therefore be defined as "As amazing as Vamazz," "What Vamazz finds amazing," or, possibly, the verily very specific "Vamazz's amazingness."

The smallest minority of all is of the opinion that Vamazz himself originated the term for the reasonable reason that no sufficient superlative previously existed that began with "V." Since, however, this minority is in Vamazz's employ and knows better than to run his tongue, this final theory will never gain traction. In a few years, it will be lost to the Sands of Time and subsequently used as a litter box.

Warm, cloth-covered arms scooped beneath the Clockmaker, rolling him face-up and supporting him under knees and back. The Clockmaker moaned and covered his eyes with the heels of his palms, too miserable to want to see or feel or acknowledge anything.

"Oof, you're heavy," Vamazz said. "How much do you weigh?"

The Clockmaker did not know and, right then, he did not care. But as Vamazz began to walk, something changed in the Clockmaker's heart. It had been many years since anyone had carried him. In fact, his only memories of it were from when he had been very young, nothing more than heart, brain, and ears—no, before that, when he was nothing but heart. His father had carried him just so, caressing him and saying what a fine piece of work he was, what magnificent craftsmanship, that he was beyond anything his father had ever created before or had ever thought to create.

But as the boy had gained limbs and torso and jaw, he had

grown too heavy for his father to carry. Since then, no one had even tried to pick him up. The closest anyone had come was Time, who had dragged him mercilessly away from the dust of everything he had ever known. *She* had not found him heavy—but then, to Time, 583 pounds is no weightier than 5.83.

"Five hundred eighty-three," mused Vamazz. "You and natural bristle paintbrushes. Both making messes." He had to stop grumbling after that—"I *beg* your pardon, I was not *grumbling*"—in order to navigate the egress from the Wasteland of Writer's Block. This egress, different every time, today involved pushing through a screaming, shouting, singing, shushing crowd of every-colored dots. That is to say that every dot was every color at once, not that every dot was a different color. They were quite painful to look at, if your eyes weren't meant to simultaneously see pumpkin and purple and puce, green and gold and goose, red and rose and roost. Vamazz's weren't, and his eyes blazed with turquoise light, but he didn't pause. Rather, he stuck out his elbows and pushed and shoved and forced his way through the dots and onto the high-stimulating train that awaited them: the Reorient Express.

By secret ways known only to the most dauntless diviners, Vamazz found a pair of empty seats on the packed train and plopped the Clockmaker down next to him.

The Clockmaker regarded him with vamazement. During their journey out of the Wasteland, he had been able to see nothing of his rescuer save masses of sapphire hair, a burnt-orange-and-blue robe, a frilly white shirt, and a hint of amethyst choker. He now observed that the masses of blue hair sprouted from the wonderful wizard's head in the usual manner, matched by extravagant eyelashes and rather thin high-arched brows.

Beyond that, his rescuer looked almost Perpetuan, or the caricature of one. The visible skin of his ivory face was, perhaps, unusually smooth, and the shape of his head unusually diamond. His wide lips were thin, his nose soft rather than razor. His shoulders spread very broad and were made broader still by blue pauldrons twice the size of his head and nearly the same color as his hair. Chains descended from these and wrapped around his waist as a belt. He'd removed his tall, triangular hat and put it on his feet, but the Clockmaker saw that it too was much the color of his hair and drooping with chains that ended in little flames. From his back gushed sparks of blue and burnt-orange flames that might have spread into wings at any moment. No heat rushed from them, however, and the fuzzy-clothed seats of the train remained unsinged.

Then the Clockmaker met Vamazz's eyes, intense under the thin brows, and knew this man could not be a Perpetuan, for he had a turquoise mind.

MEN WITH TURQUOISE MINDS:

Since the—

"Do you know what that means?" Vamazz interrupted.

"Sir?"

"Or who I am?"

The Clockmaker shook his head, ashamed at his ignorance.

"I," said Vamazz, "am Vamazz the Vamazing, superior sorcerer, excellent enchanter, awesome augurer, mediocre magician, dauntless diviner, nervy necromancer, thupreme thaumaturge, and—well, a whole lot of other titles that I can see wouldn't mean anything to you. I am also your rescuer."

"Oh," said the Clockmaker, attempting to digest this and feeling compelled to respond in kind. "I am the Clockmaker. My father, the Clockmaker, created me and sent me here to get an imagination. I have been collecting pieces of imagination for one year, two months, three weeks, four days, five hours, and six-and-a-half minutes, but Imaginarium is so big I do not know how I will ever finish. And I lost my anvil box, so I have only this one, which is already full." He unlocked his gut to show Vamazz the iron box within.

Without asking—astonishing alchemists don't ask—Vamazz took the iron box, opened it—and, exclaiming, slammed it shut again.

"What is it?" the Clockmaker asked in alarm, craning his neck.

Vamazz muttered a few words that might have been mystical or might have been merely vulgar, reopened the iron box, and showed him the fleshy soup of Despair floating with a few bloody chunks of dissolving matter.

"I do not understand," the Clockmaker said.

"I do," said Vamazz, and demonstrated his astonishing powers once again by reaching over the Clockmaker and sliding up the train window on the first attempt. Flipping the box shut with one hand, he hurled it outside.

The Clockmaker gave a cry of distress and made to push past Vamazz, presumably to jump off the train in pursuit of his box, but the superior sorcerer stopped him with one hand and, with the other, handed him an empty box.

It was the same box. The Clockmaker examined it under his strongest magnifying lens and recognized every swirl of his father's style. Only, this box looked either perfectly restored or newly made, as if Time had never worn it and Despair never soiled it.

The Clockmaker clutched the box to his chest, heart overflowing. Gone was Despair, yes, but gone also were Hypotheses, Extrapolations, Empathies, Self-Awarenesses, Creations, Inspirations, and all the rest. Nothing inhabited the box except air, and that which rode in on air's molecules.

Empty, the Clockmaker found himself left with nothing but the memory and love he'd had all along. The lust for more and more imagination, which had driven him these past months, fell pale and ghastly in its death throes and twitched once before stilling forever.

Though unable to weep, the Clockmaker curled upon himself and shook; and though not seeing tears, Vamazz wrapped his arms around him and waited.

Oblivious to everything else, the Clockmaker poured out his life story to Vamazz. Not his life story as a narrator might have told it, full of adventure and alliteration and elaborate description, but a life of love and relationships and simple moments. "And now I have failed him his last request," he gasped. "If only I had contented myself to a single hydrangea—a single brick—I might have done what he asked!"

"My dear boy," said Vamazz, "you don't know what you're talking about. I've been following your path of destruction throughout the land, with the intention of telling you off—that's how I found you—and you've been collecting everything except what you came for. Muck and nonsense! Besides, you haven't failed because you haven't yet left Imaginarium. We haven't even switched from the orange line! Come with me."

Vamazz stood, sapphire hair brushing the train lights and sparking alarmingly. Since the Clockmaker had last been in a state to observe, the every-colored dots had alighted *off* the train and small translucent lizards, naked except for green ties and indigo briefcases, had alighted *on*. These lizards studiously avoided the majestic magus's gaze, for they were train dragons, and all train dragons know that they make excellent fried snacks.

Beyond the passengers, the train looked not unlike the tram the Clockmaker had ridden in the Antechamber, save that it was rather cleaner and had blue cloth seats instead of beige plastic.

The Reorient Express blew a brief hail to Vamazz as it slowed to a complete stop. It sighed with relief as its doors slid open and the travelers minded the gap on the way out—and sighed with even more relief as it sped on immediately lest the nervy necromancer think to climb back on. Train dragons weren't the only ones who tasted good deep-fried.

The Clockmaker took in his new surroundings with dismay. He and Vamazz stood on a narrow patch of weedy grass in a quagmire of burping, farting, nose-blowing swamp. "Why are we *here?*" he asked.

"Oh, no you don't," Vamazz told the Stench firmly. "Go find someone else to bother. Hmm?" He returned his attention to the Clockmaker. "Ah! Your box, boy. Fill it here."

The Clockmaker clutched his gut closed.

Vamazz rolled his eyes. "This stuff is the Stuff of Imagination!" he explained. "Raw imagination, capable of growing into anything. Everything you've seen or made in Imaginarium was once what you see before you here. What you want isn't the prepackaged garbage you've been playing around with; it's primordial ooze. True, ooze takes longer and more effort to develop, but you'll end up with a higher-quality product and one ideally personalized to you. You could have spent a lifetime collecting plants and bones and never had enough, but a drop of this is plenty—let alone an entire box. Go on, fill it up. But this time, leave space for Hope."

The Clockmaker considered. He no longer had Extrapolations or Hypotheses to help him, but nor did he have Suspicions, and his gyroscopic heart naturally spun with purity and trust. He therefore knelt on the island, opened the box, and scooped it two-thirds full of ooze. Being the meticulous man he was, he then spent half an hour polishing the outside of the box clean with grass and Vamazz's proffered handkerchief before returning the box to his gut.

"I do not feel any different," he observed, standing up. "Although I now realize that I have permitted myself to become abominably filthy."

"The process will be slower than using prepackaged imagination," Vamazz said, "and more organic. You will feel the difference in time. Well?"

"Well what?"

"Well, where do you want to go next? What do you want to do?"

The Clockmaker frowned and tocked his head. Slime sloshed in his gut box. "I do not know," he said slowly. "I have accomplished everything I have been told to do."

"In that case," said Vamazz, "you need to learn how to think for yourself." Without asking for affirmation, he held out his hand and tilted it sharply, crying, "Votican! Blibble! Hop! Vamazz!"

The Clockmaker disappeared in a flare of turquoise light and a gentle *fwoop*. When the Stench swiggled up to investigate, it found only Vamazz remaining.

The superior sorcerer shook his head. He heightened his hands, presumably to proclaim magical proclamations, then paused pointedly as the awareness of witnesses worried his magnificent mane. "Do you *mind?*" he asked.

5

The Tomb of Ego

Utter darkness enclosed the Clockmaker. His eyes could pick out fine filigree by starlight, if held within a cubit of his face, but they could not function without some form of light. Since it had never occurred to either the Clockmaker or his father to install a head-lamp, he was left to his other senses: hearing, touch, and imagination.

Hearing assured the Clockmaker that he was quite alone. No rats brewed conspiracies in corners; no fleshy being snored its dreams to life. There *was* an almost-sound, almost like the grind of machinery. The Clockmaker, never having had much imagination before, did not now think he was imagining a sound where there was none, and yet it was so faint, so liminal, that he could not have identified for certain whether it was actual machinery or merely the grumbling of the earth.

As he felt his way around the space, rotating to project into every corner—to floor and to ceiling—the Clockmaker sang a song from his father's childhood. His sense of touch remained too rudimentary for him to rely on it for detail, but the echoes of his voice ascertained and assured him of a number of calculations: he stood in a room or cell or pit twenty steps in circumference but vastly deep. The exit must be above his reach, likely although not necessarily in the ceiling.

Assuming there *was* an exit and that Vamazz the Vamazing had not, through accident or design, dumped him in an oubliette to be forgotten—and without even a polishing cloth for company.

The Clockmaker proceeded to determine a variety of other elements to his satisfaction. He determined that the stone-and-dirt walls, when knocked upon, gave up no evidence of hollowness; that he could not climb the walls—for, apart from his not being built to climb, jump, or perform calisthenics, the walls crumbled under his fingers when he dug handholds, and he could not trust them to support him when he was high enough to be crushed by a fall; and that digging horizontally would likely be unfruitful unless he dug so far that the natural curvature of the planet brought him to the surface.

Escaping would therefore take imagination. That sense had been equally active with his hearing and touch, and he obeyed its dictates and began digging. He dug out a section of wall as tall as he was—he did not crawl well—and as deep as the breadth of his shoulders. Then he turned sideways and began digging along the wall of the pit and upward. In this way, the tunnel steadily gained height as it spiraled around the inside of the pit. One side of the tunnel remained always open to the pit, which allowed him to dump loose dirt and rock onto the floor beyond his tunnel.

On his first circuit, the Clockmaker found he had made a mistake, for the tunnel did not rise steeply enough, and he nearly walked out onto air. He had to stop and pack dirt and rocks back into the tunnel to support his upward progress. After that, instead of dumping the loose material onto the pit floor, he pressed as much of it as possible back into the tunnel behind him, to support him on his next circuit. He stopped every thirteen hours or so to wind himself up; otherwise, only his changing position marked the time.

Digging in darkness with no one to talk to and not much to hear, the Clockmaker entertained himself by strengthening his imagination. There were two particular areas he wanted to develop: clock making and poetry. Specifically, he wanted to create original clock designs and compose original poetry. He had the necessary knowledge for both in dinghy-loads, but none of the skill—and the one did not automatically transmogrify into the other. Finding the right words for a rhyme requires practice and knack, and designing the face of a watch requires visualization. But the Clockmaker was determined and industrious and, furthermore—despite his determination, industriousness, and ability to lift his own weight in stone—had many, many days of digging ahead of him.

In the first hours, the most he could manage was infinitesimal variations on established themes. He had once built a watch face decorated with tiny diamonds forming the buffalo constellation. What if he used different stones? Or a different constellation? With practice, he managed to combine these elements and hypothesize a turtle constellation in emerald. With daring, he even considered a turtle constellation in amethyst, although this made him distinctly uncomfortable, for turtles are seldom purple and never amethyst.

It took him days more to consider cutting the stones into slightly different shapes, and never during his dig did he tread on such treacherous ground as an entirely original constellation design or an abstract representation of what it meant to *be* constellation. But it was a start.

Poetry burst off the block with far more confidence and dove directly into the deep end—for the poets he'd known had not only lauded creative creation but demonstrated it at every turn, with plenty of (often contradictory) tricks and tips and training exercises for building poetic chops and imaginatic muscles. Yet by Day 43, the Clockmaker found that his inferior knowledge and understanding of poetry, as compared to clock making, gave it a distinct disadvantage.

In any case, the Clockmaker began his poetic excursion by taking a morsel of famous poetry—

> To eat or not to eat,
> That's on the menu.

—and attempting to modify it. He began slightly, with:

> To drink or not to drink
> > Shots of water drops

and then moved on to a more personal, philosophical plane:

> To wind or not to wind,
> > This I ask myself:
> Whether 'tis better for clockwork to continue
> > Past the life of its maker
> Or to let his arms and legs seize
> > And by stopping, be ended?

Here he stalled out, for it did not seem right to him that he use the famous gourmet's work and style for something so inappropriately frivolous—which is to say, inedible. Having never understood the appeal of food, he knew he could not make a proper tribute, and had therefore better lay off.

One thing on which The World's Greatest Poet and The World's Even Better Poet generally agreed was that most really spectacular poetry originated in passion. Rather than attempt to write what he did not understand or what did not fit, then, the Clockmaker supposed he should find a topic about which he was passionate.

The Clockmaker dug and thought, thought and dug, and reflected that though he had lived nearly as many years as his father had before building the gyroscopic tourbillon heart, he had a paucity of passion to draw upon. On the one hand, he had refused to become attached to the O'clocks; on the other, he had lacked the imagination to blame them for his father's death. He didn't even blame Time, particularly, any more than he would have blamed a clock for ticking. If anything, he had been grateful for the strange and uncharacteristic inclination that had spared his father's life for more than a decade—

> Nimble fingers, kindly hands
> > (second hands, minute hands)

Fleshy encasement, organ wheels
(main wheels, escape wheels)

—Stop. The Clockmaker didn't want to think of these things or of anything attached to his childhood. He could not forget, but he ruthlessly buried his first original fragment of poetry and turned instead to designing a pocket watch with only an ordinary and rather weak tourbillon of light aluminum that was almost totally ineffective at forbidding gravity dominion over the pallet fork, balance wheel, and hairspring.

This design, purposefully dreadful, was his first original clock-work invention. He never did build it. Despite himself, he had a Perpetuan's disgust for squandering time, as such a watch must have done.

The Clockmaker's tunnel bonked its head on solid rock. While it was recovering dizzily from the concussion, the Clockmaker dug his hand into the wall, stretched precariously, and pushed the ceiling grate open. It had no lock, for the builders had never supposed anyone could climb up to it. Its only *raison d'être* was to prevent anyone falling in by accident, the better to push prisoners in on purpose.

The Clockmaker had not found any bones, but there were other reasons for *that.*

As below, the Clockmaker remained in utter darkness. By touch and sound, he ascertained that two paths diverged in the stony tunnel. No breath of air differentiated them, but the Clock-maker's spinning heart told him about the tunnel's slight slant. If he was deep underground, sense would have him head uphill. But the Clockmaker had lately added imagination to sense and, with imagination, curiosity. He had absolutely no reason to believe there was any benefit to walking downhill except the possibility that this place did not operate with any reference to reason. One thing was certain, though: if uphill was the way out and he went uphill, he would never know what was downhill from him.

And so he went down.

He moved cautiously, his knowledge of metals informing him of how the grates might have decayed over time, and his imagination picturing a grate carelessly left open and what would happen to his fine metal casing if he were to fall through. His perfect memory categorized every lump and bump in the wall and every slight turn and twist of the passage.

Down he went and down for days, until he was far lower than his prison had lain. He called out every time he passed a grate, but no one ever answered his call. As he walked, the sound that might have been machinery grew, as did the cold and the damp. The passage ended in a set of stairs that the Clockmaker descended until his foot landed with a splash.

He backed up immediately and felt about. The stairs, which had been extremely narrow, abruptly spread out. He sang, and the echoes traveled exceedingly far out before returning to him and others didn't return at all, having been eaten by hungry water.

HUNGRY WATER:

Contrary to its name, hungry water is actually a plasma-based life form. Nearly transparent and closer to liquid than jelly, hungry water organisms may be identified and differentiated from water by any one of three attributes:

1) High levels of conductivity and their resulting magnetic field, which hungry water uses to make itself attractive to prey. This may result in a creeping feeling of hairs raising on the back of one's neck or of the unlikely possibility of an imminent lightning storm beneath the earth.

2) Globules of fat inevitably suspended 20% below the surface of *aqua esuriens*, fat being one of the few substances that hungry water is unable to metabolize. This fat is, incidentally, the cause of most intelligent

species' deaths from hungry water, since it is extremely useful in the Furnace of Arcana, the king of alchemical digestion.

3) The feeling of being in an infinitely large space.
This phenomenon derives from the way that hungry
water eats any sound wave with which it comes in
contact and even, in some cases, snatches sound
waves out of the air.

Hungry water exists only deep within the earth
and is seldom encountered except by super cave expe-
ditioners and foolhardy alchemists. It is therefore
mainly popular among children who have tired of having floors that are merely lava. . . .

The Clockmaker stopped and considered. He did not like the
way his heart felt—and indeed, it was as if his entire body were leaning toward the sump. He hastily stepped back, wondering what to
do next. He had no idea how far the water stretched or how deep it
became, and although he was in theory waterproof to thirty fathoms, in practice he did not quite like to test this. Besides, what if the
water were more than thirty fathoms deep?

The Clockmaker stepped back again, and nearly tripped as
something twined around his ankles and
then paused, tip barely brushing his
knee. He bent to touch the animal,
which briefly arched under his hand
before sliding away.

"Greetings, Your Highness," the
Clockmaker said. This was out-
rageous flattery, of course. The time
cats—he had met them often, for they came to
refill the Sands of Time when they heard him
sifting—had taught him that all cats were
noble beings and ought to be addressed as
such and not as either the infantilizing "kitty"

or the workmanship "O cat." But the Clockmaker didn't know whether this particular feline, which felt like it had extremely developed shoulders, almost no hair, and only four legs, should be addressed as "my lord" or "my lady" or "your grace" or "your worship" or "your dignity" or "your cool awesome stylishness."

Fortunately, no self-aggrandizing cat—which is to say, no cat—will sink from elevating himself to highness or majesty or imperial worshipfulness or ruler of the universe, given one eighth of a chance.

This particular puss pulsated, as if postulating the possibility of a purr.

"I am the Clockmaker," said the Clockmaker. "Your Highness, do you know a way across this water? I do not know how deep it runs and fear I will leak."

The cat evaporated like steam. The Clockmaker waited, but it did not bump him again or purr or yowl or scratch. His reaching hand could not find it or his conciliatory words reconstitute it.

Disappointed but unsurprised by this capriciousness from a king of capers, the Clockmaker returned his attention to the water. He did not want to go backwards until he absolutely had to, and there was no denying that weeks of digging his way out of a pit preceded by months in Imaginarium had left him in excellent condition to win any filthiness competition he cared to enter, provided the Stench wafting off him didn't dissolve the judges first.

The Clockmaker suddenly felt revolted with himself. He could not, must not continue with the apple pie filling of muck encrusted in his engraving, the mold of femurs of connecting clues clinging to the soles of his feet, the lipstick of consumeristic restlessness smeared on his elbows, and the coal dust of the Forge of Forging Ideas turning his shine matte. Then, of course, there was the heavy coat of dirt from his digging, and though its—the coat's—elbows were patched and its hem threadbare, it clung to the stuff of imagination with the fervor of dirt that might otherwise never bask in the light of day.

The Clockmaker lurched forward. He expected to hit the water in two steps, but it lurked nearly four paces distant, and felt oddly thin—as if it had picked up its skirts to let him pass but missed a few dangling shreds of taffeta. Liquid enveloped the Clockmaker's feet, ankles, shins, knees, thighs, and abdomen. A slight current tugged on him as it passed his heart, but gravity had a firmer hold than magnetism on his quarter ton, and he kept on.

Being submerged was not as the Clockmaker had expected. Some part of him had felt sure that water would press in on him from every side, threatening the integrity of his casing. Instead, this water tugged at him magnetically—not strongly enough to threaten his integrity in the opposite way, but strongly enough to make him uncomfortable. Then there was the sharp feeling that sometimes sparked through him, which he did not like but which did not harm him—although if his father had invested in newfangled batteries and electrical impulses instead of good, reliable winding mechanisms and unadulterated clockwork, the Clockmaker might have been in trouble. On the other hand, at least the streaking forks of lightning sizzling by him let him see in flashes.

He went deeper, unhesitating but minding the angle of his feet, until the surface hovered too far above to feel. Hardly had he gone twice as deep as he was tall than his feet turned upward again—for the lake was only 0.633 miles at its widest point.

In the time it took a minute hand to tick to 13 twice more, the Clockmaker's head surfaced, quickly followed by the rest of him— significantly cleaner and less wet than might be expected, for the water trailed wriggling snakes down his casing rather than be sepa- rated from its body. He put one foot on dry land and then another and walked obliviously off, thus becoming the first being in the mul- ti-verse ever to traverse the hungry water without protection and yet emerge unscathed.

The truth was, the hungry water hadn't even known he was there until it felt him splashing out. It had been distracted toward the Clockmaker's ten o'clock by its most enduring and pestiferous ene- my. Nearly every day, that disreputable feline pranced about its shoreline, yowling the song of its people, just out of reach—and nearly every day, the hungry water lunged and splashed at it, desperate for a taste.

Obsession with the cat thundered through the hungry water's consciousness. It would have done anything to eat that cat. It had touched it once—once! But the cat had batted it away and levitated nine feet straight up onto a ledge before it could get a grip. On this particular occasion, it struck the hungry water that the cat's wicked waltz was a touch more careless than usual, and it pursued the creature with more than usual ferocity.

Only when the cat broke into thousands of shivering shards of laughter did the enraged hungry water feel metal feet pulling out of its shallows and realize it had been tricked.

As the Clockmaker strode away from the lake, a howl of disappointed hunger echoed up after him, making rocks quake and soil shake, worms tremble and torms wremble. It knocked moles about in their tunnels and discombobulated a family of foxes. It traveled up through strands of grass to a cotton-eyed Joe, who immediately went insane and ran off to battle the house centipede that had been peacefully eating a house and hadn't in the least expected such opposition.

Within the tunnels snaking away from the hungry water lake, the Clockmaker caught himself to avoid stumbling, the cat sniggered, and something that had been sleeping, woke.

Assuming that earth-shatteringly vast howls were par for the course for this part of the world, the Clockmaker continued merrily along his way. The makeshift bath had raised his spirits amazingly. And he hadn't leaked! And here was a screw stair handily situated to elevate him!

He began ascending immediately, ignoring the spiders swarming around him, though he deplored the way their webbing clung to his clean casing. The spiders in turn broke their teeth on metal and squandered mammoth-felling venom on an insensible target.

Up the Clockmaker stepped and up for days, clockwork legs never tiring, keen ears never catching the uneven shuffle of footsteps following him. He passed from the sixth sublevel to the fifth to the fourth (where his prison pit sank, albeit several miles distant) to the third. The second sublevel had gotten up and migrated centuries ago, but the Clockmaker didn't know what he was missing. In the first sublevel, the Clockmaker found signs of life—as could only be expected by anyone in the least familiar with the Tomb of Ego the Maniac.

EGO THE MANIAC:

Supreme Ruler of the Universe for less than a fortnight, Ego is nowadays primarily remembered for his contributions to internment, including such studies as entombment, urnology, columbariums, mycology, and architecture. When asked why he didn't approve of cremation, Ego's fiery retort shriveled fifty reporters in one sentence. Many militaries have since attempted to recreate the phrase, without success.

Some historians theorize that the reason Ego lasted such a short stretch as Supreme Ruler of the Universe was that he expended all his resources building himself a tomb, but others call this improbable, citing his intense brain power—

|Cross-reference, MANIACS: Beings whose only organ is their brain, maniacs must necessarily convince or enslave others to do their bidding. Their powers include every tele (telepathy, telekinesis, teleportation, etc.). The most notable maniac was Supreme Ruler of the Universe Ego. . . . |

—and terrific age. Ego, they say, must have known he

was about to die, and in fact took the seat of Supreme Ruler of the Universe specifically to build a suitably staggeringly striking monument to himself. . . .

"Down With Life!" signs proclaimed. "Ego is too amazing for life! Follow his example!" "Life is passé!" Running lights arrowed to the Clockmaker's right, and a large-print posting gave him specific instructions on how he could sacrifice himself to show solidarity with Ego.

Led by some compulsion he didn't understand, the Clockmaker followed the arrows to the edge of a cliff and looked down. Scoring on the sides demonstrated that it had once been so full that new pilgrims had no longer found the drop fatal. Since then, however, it had been picked as clean as the prison pit.

What a great pity, the Clockmaker thought, *that the tomb has been so disrespectfully emptied. What villain could have done such a thing? Ego deserved every sacrifice made in his honor. Every sacrifice in the world.* And if tomb robbers had acted so appallingly, then at least the Clockmaker could begin a new pile. He robotically stretched one leg over the side of the cliff and—

And stopped and hurried backwards. Where had *that* come from? He'd never even heard of Ego the Maniac before!

Yes, but he must have been a very great leader, to have such a tomb, whispered the telepathic echoes of days deceased. The Clockmaker must love him, must obey him.

"I am a living being, and I am art," the Clockmaker said aloud, to drown out the whispers. "I was sent here to learn how to think for my*self*." Turning sharply to leave, he ran straight into the creature that had been stalking him since the hungry water had woken it.

It stumbled back and fell in a jumble of limbs, mostly out of surprise. In the space of a tick, its giant mantis legs rotated in their sockets and righted it.

Looming over the Clockmaker, the creature hinged and unhinged its jaw, mindless hunger slavering between its teeth, rolling shoulders popping in and out of alignment as it prepared a pounce.

KHEIR:

A mutant of *ursus horribilis*, the kheir migrated underground after every chiropractor in the universe appealed to Supreme Ruler Ego for a restraining order. While they sympathized with its predicament (it must be truly painful and annoying to have every single joint in your body constantly dislocating and relocating), eating them was completely out of line.

The kheir lunged at the Clockmaker, and he had to move very swiftly indeed to duck out of its way. "Stop!" he cried. "I mean you no harm!"

The kheir lashed out and struck the Clockmaker's middle with such tremendous force that the Clockmaker flew across the floor and into a sign, denting his casing, cracking two delicate bridges, and ripping a cable.

As the Clockmaker cried out in distress, the kheir picked up speed. An instant before it fell upon him, the Clockmaker threw himself aside and blurred away. He ran as he had not run even in Time's palace, through the sublevel and up the broad stairs beyond. He left the kheir far behind, his heavy metal footsteps echoing through the tomb.

Behind him, the kheir skidded to a halt, then rearranged its joints. It had pursued the Clockmaker for days, and knew it could follow his clanging, clamoring vibrations anywhere.

The Clockmaker emerged into sunlight. It rayed down through tiny skylights far above, illuminating monuments that Ego had built to himself, complete with multitudinous descriptions of his own greatness. Dominating the first level stood a statue of Ego himself, a tremendous brain so large that a child could hide in the details of the cerebellum. Ego had, in fact, meant that his entire tomb be a replica of his brain, but the mountain had sadly been the wrong shape and he had, in any case, died before it was complete.

The Clockmaker saw the brain, as he saw everything, but he didn't pause to dwell on the details. He whizzed past, to a set of portcullises built to protect the glorious Ego from tomb robbers . . . but mostly used to prevent the things that lurked beneath from escaping.

The Clockmaker zipped up to the first portcullis and flung the lever. The portcullis, balanced with weights and counterweights and clockwork, rose easily. The Clockmaker flung himself beneath it and grabbed the lever on the other side. But instead of the exterior portcullis opening, the interior one closed with a spin of clockwork gears and a clang of steel spikes sinking into their stone grooves.

He didn't have time for this. He could see fabulous freedom beyond the second portcullis—and hear the kheir not far behind him. He grabbed the bars of the outer portcullis and heaved upward.

"It won't work," said a surprisingly deep, round contralto.

Where no one had been before, a cat sat beyond the outer portcullis, in the fresh morning air. Languid sunlight bathed her bony, nearly hairless form and settled between muscular shoulders.

"These portcullises," the cat went on, "were designed to trap and hold creatures far stronger than you."

"Please," said the Clockmaker, "push the lever. Let me out."

The cat tucked her tail around her legs scornfully. "Why should I?"

"Because that monster is going to kill me!"

"I know the kheir wants to," the cat said, "but what concern is that of mine?"

The Clockmaker wasn't sure how to answer this. He had never come across such a sentiment before, or not since gaining the imagination to understand it.

As he hesitated, the kheir swung into view, massive limbs rolling and roiling in its uneven gait. It spotted him and shrieked in triumph, its voice echoing around the chamber and frolicking in the cavities of the giant brain.

"See it from my point of view," said the cat. "In order to rescue you, I'd have to stand up, walk over there, and push the lever. That would take effort, and I am an incredibly lazy creature."

The kheir slowed as it approached the portcullises and

unsheathed its two front wrists. Bony serrations protruded from each forearm, deadly and effective as hacksaws. The Clockmaker eyed them fearfully as the kheir brought them to the inner portcullis bars to saw and scrape, raw and rack, craaaw and krrrk. Sparks flew and smoke grew and the cat only pretended not to cringe at the hideous racket and the even more hideous kheir bear.

"Please," the Clockmaker begged, craning his neck in an attempt to simultaneously watch both cat and kheir, "was it not you I met down by the lake?"

The cat looked mysterious.

"That was a long way away! If you have come so far, you cannot be that lazy!"

"You have a point," the cat said, stretching her spine and repuddling herself. "I have already rescued you once, from the hungry water. A whim, and one that puts you in my debt. But what was the point, if you're just going to keep getting in mortal danger?"

The Clockmaker dredged up his memories of the time cats. He didn't remember this cat having saved him, but wasn't about to quibble now, with the kheir halfway through the first bar. "If I die now," he said, "I will not be able to fulfill my obligation to you."

"True," said the cat. "Still, it seems an awful lot of effort."

The scratching on the bars increased for a frenetic few seconds and then ceased. As the Clockmaker watched, the kheir folded its joints outward, flattening arms to its back like grasshopper wings and pressing itself against the bars until its fat bulged through and its neck craned and its scaly skin—devoid of hair after millennia beneath the earth—rasped against metal.

"Oh please!" the Clockmaker cried. "Hurry!"

"I don't like being hurried," the cat observed. "And I think I should be paid back for your first debt before you incur any more. But I see you are in no position to pay. Hmm."

The kheir screamed with frustration as it stuck and fought to pull itself back out and free. The weakened bars bent as it slooped out, but they did not crack—yet.

"I know!" the cat cried. "We'll have a game of riddles!"

"I am sorry," the Clockmaker said, confusion joining terror. "I do not understand. I have played games but never heard of riddles."

"What? Impossible! What an idiot. Who hasn't heard of riddles? They're—oh, it's too much work to explain it to you! You know what a poem is, I hope?"

"I do," the Clockmaker replied, trying to hide how hopeful he suddenly felt despite the kheir setting its saw arm to the next bar and filling the air with metal filings. There weren't many topics on which he felt confident, but he could discuss poetry all day.

"Then we'll have a poetry contest," the cat said. "If you have the better poem, I will let you out."

"That seems fair," said the Clockmaker. "And if I do not?"

The cat smiled smugly, whiskers poking out. "Then you will provide me with entertainment in your dying moments."

This struck the Clockmaker as particularly unpleasant—but, after all, the cat had chosen poetry. He should be able to win. "I agree," he said, pulling in his focus. Afraid though he was, he knew he would need every second hand, every torsion spring of his attention for this. The kheir would come through too soon or not—there was nothing he could do about *that.*

"Excellent," said that cat. "I'll go first. Ahem:

"I stand before the mirror, close enough
To touch the gleaming surface, feel the chill
Of brass beneath my fingers. This, the stuff
I labor over, day and night—yet still
Intrudes upon my mind. This want, this heat:

63

Alive, not breathing. Heart is beating true,
In perfect time. A miracle, a feat
Beyond my skill. I admire, flatter you,
Await your notice. Worse than hope, despair
Oppresses me. Stay with me, beloved, trust.
Am I not good enough? Why won't you care?
But what does wailing alter? Life's not just.
So I'll repair your heart with my own heart
And smile farewell as it splits me apart."

The Clockmaker had frozen in place during this recitation, heart spinning, mind screaming. He had never heard the poem before, but he knew who had written it. Who had sat with him for so many hours while The World's Greatest Poet taught him about sonnets, the highest form of poetry. Who had begged him to stay with her in the Antechamber.

How blind he had been, not to see how Vialia felt! And yet he had *not* seen. He had not yet traveled through Empathy and filled his iron gut box with Imagination. Oh, for those days of ignorance, that blissful state! Now, how helpless he was to salve her hurt.

"Ahem," said the cat. "Can I take your silence as a concession? The kheir is certainly about to."

The Clockmaker snapped back with a jolt. Poem! He needed a poem! But sonnets were the highest form of poetry, and the cat had already recited one!

Scraaaaaaakk.

The Clockmaker glanced back again and saw that the kheir had broken through a second bar. One more, and it could pull itself through inch by inch, and there wouldn't be anything he could do to stop it. He had to win, and quickly.

But what could he recite? Another sonnet? What sonnet did he know or could he create that would affect the cat as the cat's had affected him? Yet another type of poem would not do, for sonnets were the greatest poems in the world! How could he compose something *even better?*

Inspiration hit him with a brick. He turned a smile on the cat, freed himself from the manacles of meter and rhyme, and said:

"This is a poem.
Deal with it."

The cat looked at him. He looked at the cat. The cat licked her paw.

"Well?" the Clockmaker said.

"Well what? Oh, all right." The cat sniffed. "That's what I get for going easy on you. Fine!" She climbed languorously to her feet and padded over to push the lever. "But you still owe me!"

Then the cat disappeared, grin first, as the Clockmaker blurred out. He slammed the lever shut from outside, turned, and ran.

Hardly had he gone five paces, however, than the Clockmaker abruptly dug his feet in. He rocked once and stabilized a whisker away from taking a long drop and a short stop off the precipice.

To say that this precipice was nothing to sneeze at, although generally good advice regarding hygiene, would be such a vast and inexorable falsehood that any soul who truly stood for truth and justice and good grammar would feel it his indelible duty to dispose of the deplorable dictator without delay. Which is not to say the converse, that Ego the Maniac had been unreasonably extravagant in his architecture. Indeed, no Supreme Ruler of the Universe had ever deserved more or ever-so-stylishly executed his just deserts with fork or spoon than Ego. The extremeness of this precipice was not excessive, because only extremeness was worthy of a Supreme Ruler of the Universe.

And extreme it was. You could cut a blackberry cheesecake on its edge without wasting a glob of filling—or smash a round of brie on its side for a perfect grated topping. Falling stones, clouds, and clockwork men would shatter with marvelous tinkling chimes on the orchestra of spikes below, if any could get high enough to make the attempt.

Before Ego's rise to fame, daredevil rock-climbing sororities had announced the summit unscaleable and shaken their heads in sad reproach when some brash young know-it-all proclaimed she would prove them wrong.

Then Ego, as Supreme Ruler of the Universe, proclaimed it his final resting place with the tele powers of his vast brain, and the pilgrims found a way.

They came in ones and twos, in sevens and nines and forty-threes, in droves and clans and daredevil rock-climbing sororities. They came familiar with the mountain's repute and steeped in the over-brewed oolong of ignorance. They mostly helped one another ascend, drilling anchors into the rock face and planting specially reinforced soles against its razor-pimpled skin and grasping rope woven from the entrails of the infamously mournful gruwyrm.

So enduring, so awesome were these materials that even now, three thousand years later, pilgrims could scale the rock face—and scale it some still did, despite the intervening Supreme Rulers of the Universe's cries for cessation. On they came, drawn by the telepathic echoes, their own hubris, and the traditions of their sororities.

But no one had designed the latticework of ropes for climbing *down*.

Inside the outer portcullis, the kheir paced. It could not pass through—the restraining order saw to that—but it could wait, for its prey had nowhere else to go.

"Cat!" cried the Clockmaker. "Honorable feline, majestic majesty—where am I to go? Will you not return and help me?"

The cat would not, and the Clockmaker was left to contemplate his options. Even had he known the climbing equipment was there, which he did not, he was too familiar with his own abilities to delude himself into attempting to use it; he might as well throw himself off the precipice and hope he learned to fly halfway down. Returning through the portcullis hardly seemed a more attractive option, however, and trickery was too foreign to his nature to be learned even in Imaginarium. What, then?

There wasn't much to investigate up here: the landing existed only directly before the portcullis, fifteen feet out and thirty across, with neatly squared edges. Beyond it, the mountain rose and fell with its habitual rudeness.

He could not climb up; he could not climb down; he could not go back. That left waiting, perhaps for centuries, high up where wind and rain and snow and hail and sun could wear at him with more variance but equal certainty as time.

The Clockmaker was patient, but this option did not appeal to him, so he cupped his hands around his mouth and began yelling: "Help! Help! Help! Help! Help! Help! Help! Help! Help! Help! Help! Help! Help!"

"Help what?" asked Vamazz the Vamazing, using an ancient gruwyrm rope to lever himself over the edge. He wore his full armor in sapphire blue, and his matching hair poofed bigger than ever, but you'd have thought by his tone that he'd just happened to be in the neighborhood when he'd heard the Clockmaker and thought he might as well investigate as not. "I just happened to be in the neighborhood," he explained. "When I heard you, I thought I might as well investigate as not. What seems to be the matter?" He frowned. "Have we met? You seem familiar."

This memory lapse struck the Clockmaker as astonishing and hurtful, even for a fleshy being. "It is your fault that I am here!" he accused.

Vamazz hummed, considered this, and dismissed it with a shake. "I have never sent a metal man to the mouth of this Tomb."

"No, sir, but seventy-four days, fourteen hours, three minutes, and ten seconds ago, you sent me to a pit inside the mountain. Do you not recall? You rescued me! We were in Imaginarium, and I had succumbed to Despair. You helped me fill my iron gut box with Imagination, and you told me that you would send me somewhere I could learn to think for myself."

"And have you learned to think for yourself?" Vamazz asked, sounding interested.

"I am not sure," the Clockmaker admitted. "I believe I have only begun. But you did not need to send me into that prison!"

"Be fair," said Vamazz; "I didn't know you were real. Imaginarium likes to throw challenges at people, and who ever heard of a clockwork man? Besides, you escaped well enough—and last time I came here, it took some thinking for myself to bat aside the telepathic residue, so you must have thought for yourself a little." He looked the Clockmaker up and down in self-congratulation. "How you have grown since I saw you last! You *have* been exercising your imagination. I shake your hand, sir"—he did so, energetically, grinning. "How have you been enjoying it? Tell me all your adventures. No, I insist. Listening is the least I can do, having inflicted them on you. Were they *very* terrible?"

No reproach could withstand Vamazz's obvious enthusiasm, and before long, the Clockmaker found himself telling the excellent enchanter everything. Vamazz listened closely and chuckled occasionally and, though the Clockmaker didn't realize it, understood rather more than the Clockmaker himself—for Vamazz had a turquoise mind.

MEN WITH TURQUOISE MINDS:

Without doubt—

"You are in a fix," Vamazz interrupted, clapping the Clockmaker's shoulder, "and I can't help but feel partly responsible. Are you still inclined toward self-improvement?"

"I have not yet considered my future," the Clockmaker admitted.

"The first step is, of course, to get you out of here," Vamazz mused, quite as if he hadn't heard. "Let's see. Ah!" He held out his free hand, palm down. Tilting it sharply sideways, he cried, "Phalta! Ghoolash! Futavore! Vamazz!"

With a puff of turquoise smoke and a strong smell of tuna fish, the Clockmaker vanished.

6

Nindi's Dome

Magnesium hot light seared the dusty air, burning away invasive shadows and peeling apart conspiracies to learn what lay inside. Hyena-faced daisies cowered under its ferocity, and whale fat blubbered and burped up its secrets. Only the eggplants flourished under such scrutiny while remaining inscrutable, for they were more alien by far than the light—and thereby earned its uneasy respect.

The Clockmaker attempted to shade his eyes, but no shade fell from his flattened hand. He stepped away, turning, and felt something ploosh beneath his foot. He stilled, not knowing what he had stepped on; the light was so bright that he could see nothing but *it*, and he feared harming any living creature.

The light snapped off. "What manner of being is it?" someone murmured.

"Humanoid. Coated in metal plating or armor."

"Is it viable?"

"Excuse me?" called the Clockmaker, having ascertained that he had only stepped on an eggplant.

"Inconclusive at this time."

Realizing that the speakers either could not hear him or had no interest in him, the Clockmaker turned his attention elsewhere.

Without excessive light dominating his oculars, he found plenty to occupy his mind. He appeared to be in an enormous domed room, its floor a swatch of ivory dust that collected in dunes and cliques and fandoms. The dust poofed into the air with the Clock-maker's faintest twitch, and he regarded it suspiciously—for dust has been known to find its way where even water fears to go. He therefore flicked on his highest magnification and examined the dust grain by grain.

Why, this was sawdust! But by far the finest sawdust he had ever seen—finer even than the dust from sanding with 9,000-grit sandpaper inside the fish engravings of a grandmother clock; finer than was possible with any wood the Clockmaker knew of. But then, the Clockmaker had never before encountered soul wood.

SOUL WOOD:

Primarily known for the catchy rhythms, call-and-response choruses, and twirling intermediary noises it produces while drying, soul wood is extremely prized for the precision and beauty it affords woodcraft. As it unfortunately is also very fragile, the possibility of medical and military uses has largely been dismissed. . . .

Being rather near-sighted, the Clockmaker marched around the dusty room, leaning in to examine everything and massacring egg-plants by the carton-full. Whenever anything particularly caught his interest, he flipped his magnification from 1x to 10x or 50x and leaned in until his sharp nose threatened the integrity of whatever he examined.

The room had been organized into areas. The two closest to the Clockmaker involved a smooth taupe-and-maroon wall and a num-ber of darkly reflective surfaces; it was that direction from which the continuing voices trickled. He resolved to stop there last, for in his experience, living beings tended to interrupt his explorations rather than join in on them.

Once he had satisfied himself as to the nature of the sawdust and eggplants, he moved on to the clear ancestors of the sawdust: the chairs.

The Clockmaker knew nothing of chairs. He could not have said why some chairs had cushions and why some did not, or the significance of different back heights, seat contours, or leg quantities. If provided with samples of wing, egg, and birdie chairs, he could certainly have analyzed their distinctive features but not explained why these features might or might not be desirable or what was their most fashionable setting. In fact, he had very seldom seen chairs in use. There had been stools and a rather shabby sofa in his father's house and in Vialia's; and the pub he had frequented with the fluvron poets had had chairs for patrons. As for Time's palace, the chairs there had every one of them been completely unique and (for the most part) meant as a part of the general décor rather than as a practical resting place.

In his general ignorance and larval stage beauty comprehension, the Clockmaker admired every chair equally, whether it was wing or egg or birdie—which several were—or club, rocking, ancient curule, molded Bergère, open-armed fauteuil, precarious cantilever, or one of the twenty-eight other types of chair that the Clockmaker enumerated.

The further back the Clockmaker traveled, the more his admiration turned to disapproval. Mushrooms held meetings on seats; rot nibbled at legs; eggplants everythinged everywhere. Some chairs had crumbled to the point of collapse, hyena-faced daisies and vultured watermelons bending over them eagerly. Further still, he found chairs degraded until they interested nothing but oozing white worms, and beyond that—the largest dune of all, a veritable mountain of sawdust and chair backs.

For that was the curious thing: no matter the state of the rest of each chair, the back remained pristine. Age touched them not; nor did scavengers. There is something particularly pathetic about a chair back without a chair attached, but the Clockmaker was yet too young in the ways of imagination to put his finger on what.

Entirely revolted by the neglect before him, the Clockmaker turned his attention to the room's next area: the open woodshop where, presumably, the chairs were manufactured before being forgotten.

The Clockmaker had some knowledge of woodworking, as concerned clocks, and he had seen any number (but, specifically, 14) woodshops in the Antechamber. Each of those had been eccentric and specialized to the extreme, but there are some tools that no woodshop is complete without, and even from a distance, the Clockmaker could see a variety of toolboxes that might easily hold hammers and nails, screwdrivers and screws, saws and sandpaper, wrenches and pliers, levels and compasses.

The real question, of course, was whether any of these tools was precise enough to repair or create replacement parts for his cracked bridges and torn cable, or to smooth out the dents in his fine casing. It was clear to him that he could not repair himself here, surrounded by clogging sawdust, but perhaps if he could take the tools away with him . . .

Leaving a ribbon of eggplant destruction behind him, the Clockmaker arrived at the woodshop and reached for the nearest toolbox. Immediately, an alarm shrilled the air. The taupe-and-maroon wall eviscerated its darkly reflective surfaces, and engorged insects spilled out: a buzzing fly as plump as the Clockmaker's head; spindly-legged billipedes up to his knees; plodding armored beetles with antennae waving; an enormously fuzzy moth bobbing drunkenly overhead. They surrounded the Clockmaker between three and four ticks of a second hand, shouting at him:

"The subject is not permitted to touch the master's property!"

"The subject will desist immediately!"

"The subject will return to the testing area!"

And, from the moth, "Alarm! Alarm!"

The Clockmaker dropped his hand. "I do not understand," he said.

"The subject will obey!"

"The subject will not question commands!"

"The subject—"

"And what," asked a new voice, its silky tenor slicing through the shouts and letting the cut end fall to the floor, "is going on here?"

Nindi, the master of chair crafting, bug bloating, and the dome, was thin as a pole and twenty-five feet tall exactly. He wore a full metal flat-brimmed soldier's cap, and the incandescence of intelligence shone orange-gold from the four glass panels of his head—for Nindi was a lamppost. Quite a superior sort of lamppost, mind, being suitable for streets rather than just gardens and garages.

The Clockmaker had come across lampposts before many times, both in Perpetua and in the Antechamber, but these had invariably been in their hibernation stage. The Clockmaker regarded this waking lamppost with terrific interest, for lampposts, like clockwork men, are made primarily of metal.

Spotting the Clockmaker spot him, Nindi leaned forward. Unlike the planted forms of hibernating lampposts, his root feet spread around him like octopus tentacles. They swam through the sawdust, effortlessly carrying him near.

"Hello," said the Clockmaker, craning his neck as far as he was able. "May I please borrow some of your woodworking tools and a clean room? I am damaged and would repair myself."

Master Nindi leaned in so that his headlight fell full upon the Clockmaker's upturned face. "You are a curious being," he said. "I have never come across one such as you. What are you?"

This was not a question that anyone had asked the Clockmaker before. He considered briefly. "I am a living being," he said, "and I am art."

"But what is your species? Who are your people?"

"I do not believe," the Clockmaker said, upon flection and reflection, "that I have either species or people. Time commissioned me, my father the Clockmaker designed and built me, and I filled my own gut box with imagination. I am currently on a quest to discover my purpose and learn to think for myself and thereby complete my making."

"Self-actualization!" exclaimed Master Nindi to himself. "That is indicative! But being crafted—being an amalgamation of cogs and

73

springs and clockwork . . . I don't know. I just don't know."

"Know what, sir?" the Clockmaker prompted.

"Why—whether you have a soul!"

"Distilled goodness incorporates every virtue but lacks—what? Puzzle Girl?"

"The ability to act," Puzzle Girl responded obediently, eyes flicking over to meet the Clockmaker's.

"Rendering it useless," commented the winter-white pycckni dwarf hamster, who claimed his name was Raskolnikov.

"Goodness without action is only useless," countered Puzzle Girl, "if the goodness of goodness is defined by its utility."

"Without the proof that action provides," said Raskolnikov, "how do you know goodness is actually goodness or only the pretense thereof?"

"Clockmaker?" prompted Master Nindi, who always interfered if one of them wasn't talkative enough. How was he to know, he asked them, whether they had souls if he never heard what they had to say?

"I do not know," the Clockmaker admitted. "What is the default setting of goodness?"

This rather academic conversation was not set inside a chalky classroom, beneath towering bookshelves, or arranged pleasantly among the chairs. Instead, the four of them—five, if you counted Sharpig—worked in the prisoner pens as they spoke, attending to the various chores they covered between prisoner loads. Master Nindi took the task of checking the restraints, to make sure they were in good condition. He had no hands, but his shining intellect provided a powerful if limited-distance photokinesis. Being the tallest, he also checked the upper levels. The Clockmaker, as the strongest, carried out corpses and buckets of waste while Puzzle Girl swept and mopped. Raskolnikov provided running commentary as he scurried along the corners of the cells, and Sharpig ate the rotting remains of the prisoners' slop.

It was horrifying work, and the Clockmaker had not the gift of forgetfulness. However, as he had also not the curse of ever witnessing the prisoners while they were still alive—for Master Nindi shoved the Clockmaker with the other three behind a barrier of light while dragging prisoners from their pen to his Soul Chamber—the Clockmaker did his best to shepherd his imagination in other directions and cling desperately to his ignorance. He did not delude himself that he was anything but helpless against Master Nindi, whose magic was powerful indeed.

Master Nindi's four slaves were each utterly unique, according to him, but had one thing in common: he was uncertain whether they had souls. He had therefore decided to keep them close and grill them and drill them until he could determine the matter one way or the other.

The Clockmaker had eventually come to terms with his companions, but the first few weeks had been difficult. Puzzle Girl, he had found especially painful to look at, as she had been so haphazardly constructed. Unlike the Clockmaker, whose every wheel and panel had been laboriously designed, crafted, and placed with excruciating precision, Puzzle Girl had come into being largely by mistake.

"I had no awareness of being built," she explained one morning after Master Nindi had planted himself for the day. "I only pieced it together later. As I understand it, what happened was this:

"There was once a family named the Gastleys who lived in Virulence Vale city. The Gastley children—Influenza, Typhoid, Measles, Mumps, Tetanus, and Rubella—were sent by their fearful parents to live with their Uncle Nerves in the country.

"Having been raised in a big city, the Gastley children had never learned manners. When they became bored—which happened quite quickly, as Nerves had no interest in children and less in children such as these—they turned to naughtiness and pranks and, especially, to beginning a war against their neighbor, the Warty Warlock.

"They started small, with mistletoe in his tea and belladonna in his pillow, but things soon escalated. Finally, they decided to make a manikin, something to place in his living room so that when he came home, he would think a monster awaited him. Perhaps they knew this was his particular fear; later events would support that theory.

"In any case, they began to build. They emptied silverware drawers and smashed plates. They scooped out cans of boiled asparagus and jars of cashew butter and canvas bags of teff flour. They used a golf club for one leg and a can opener for the sternum, a broken lamp stand for the other leg and an umbrella skeleton for the ribs and leather belts for the tendons and rubber bands for the joints—and you can see the rest. They spent days crafting, constantly coming up with new ideas not only to improve the scare they'd give the Warty Warlock but also to cause their uncle as much bother as possible.

"Finally, the manikin was completed. That evening, when the Warty Warlock was away at an aesthetician conference, they snuck into his house and stood the manikin up in his living room, so that when he came into his house and took off his hat and turned to take off his coat, he would see it and get the scare of his life.

"Well, they succeeded—rather more than they meant to! When the Warty Warlock saw the manikin looming up out of the darkness, his heart exploded with an echoing pop that shot his magic through his chest, across the room . . . and into the manikin.

"In that moment, I was born. And I've been alive ever since."

She smiled rather sadly.

"The Gastley children were terrified of me. I only ever got Typhoid to talk to me by trapping her, which is how I know as much as I do. Soon, the whole neighborhood was hiding away from me, refusing to answer my knocks or tell me where I should go except *away*. Word of this caught Master Nindi's attention, and soon he came to pick me up and bring me here."

"Then you must be very young," said the Clockmaker.

"Oh, yes," agreed Puzzle Girl. "I have not yet lived a full year— but at the same time, I feel that I have been alive for thirty-seven. You see, I seemed to have come into existence knowing rather a lot. I think some of the magic remembered what the Warty Warlock knew, and so that knowledge is inside me."

Sharpig wasn't in the dome when the Clockmaker first arrived; Master Nindi brought him in eight days, thirty-one minutes later. The Clockmaker, Puzzle Girl, and Raskolnikov were standing among the broken chairs, listening to faintly sighed doo-waps, when Master Nindi swept in, leading a small army of giant ants and their burden: a squealing, ovular pinkish creature perhaps two cubits long and one in diameter. The ants dumped it near the taupe-and-maroon wall and then retreated to turn the magnesium light on full.

Raskolnikov immediately began swearing at the brightness, but the Clockmaker and Puzzle Girl found they could look on from this distance, and observe. Both were immensely curious at this break in pattern.

The pinkish creature rolled around on his hairy back. Under the harsh light, he stopped squealing, and his nose worked like crazy. He righted himself, and the wrinkled snout split into a massive maw overflowing with triangular teeth. Sharpig immediately set on the eggplants, tearing through thin purple flesh and swallowing chunks whole. He worked his way methodically, eating both the fetid remains of trampled eggplants and their recent replacements, not discriminating when he came to daisies and mushrooms and moss, but stopping short of the wriggling white worms.

"Why is Master Nindi allowing this destruction?" the Clockmaker wondered in alarm. "The chairs will be damaged!"

Raskolnikov regarded him in disgust. "Isn't it obvious? Nindi isn't sure whether this being has a soul—same as us."

"But," said Puzzle Girl, "it's clearly just an animal. Look at it! It doesn't even wonder where it is or how it got here; it cares about nothing but gorging itself. How could *it* have a soul?"

"You don't know anything." Raskolnikov's words were sneering, but his tone was softened by something like pity—for Puzzle

Girl, perhaps, or for Sharpig or for himself. He looked like he might be about to go speak to the new arrival, but shrank from it. A pycckni hamster is much smaller than a full-grown eggplant, and this was before they knew that no matter the temptation, Sharpig never ate meat or harmed a fleshy being—which was one of the oddities that had drawn Master Nindi's attention.

However, Raskolnikov must have approached Sharpig at some point, because the Clockmaker thereafter often saw them together, as if in conference, and because Raskolnikov told them the creature's name. In private, the Clockmaker and Puzzle Girl theorized that the hamster must be able to communicate with Sharpig because both were fleshy beings, but the truth was that Sharpig could talk quite clearly, if in a rudimentary sort of way, and did so once he was sufficiently comfortable around them.

Unfortunately, all he ever seemed to talk about was his insatiable hunger. Neither Puzzle Girl nor the Clockmaker had ever been hungry, and complained about Sharpig until Raskolnikov told them harshly to shut up.

"If you don't know what it's like to be constantly, horribly hungry," he snapped, "then you have no right to judge him."

"Do *you* know what it's like to be constantly, horribly hungry?" Puzzle Girl asked.

"I don't see how that's any business of yours," Raskolnikov replied. Then he shook his head and said, "He's told me his story, and given me permission to share it. Will you listen?"

They would. Raptly but with limited comprehension, they attended as Raskolnikov wove a harrowing tale of magico-genetic experimentation, gene splitting and jean splicing, surgery and test tubes, microbial samples and chromosomal injections.

"Sharpig's a mixture of diverse parts, as you are, Puzzle Girl—save that he is crafted of living beings instead of household miscellanea. So have some empathy. He's been through more agony than your pitiful brains can begin to fathom, and he's still in it."

The Clockmaker and Puzzle Girl did not answer. Perhaps one was remembering the disintegration of his father before his eyes and between his fingertips—and the other was remembering the way the first person ever to see her had fallen down dead in horror and that her creators had run screaming from her.

"You've been with the master longer than any of us," Puzzle Girl said to Raskolnikov, sometime later. "What's your story?"

"That," said Raskolnikov, "I'm not going to tell you. Don't ask again."

Which, Puzzle Girl commented privately to the Clockmaker, was precisely the answer she had expected.

Even before the inception of his obsession with souls, Master Nindi Vidkani enjoyed a reputation in Chinula—which was the land in whose center he had erected his dome. For, in addition to the ordinary photokinesis that all lampposts have, Nindi had the ability to alter the light he emitted in such a way as to force anyone who fell beneath its glow to tell the truth. (He had turned this ability on the Clockmaker when they'd first spoken, but as the Clockmaker always told the truth, it made no difference.) Naturally, Nindi used this ability to make money.

He went about it like this: in the evening, he traveled to a sketchy area in a sketchy part of town, such as behind the old pencil factory. There, he drilled his roots deep into the earth and mimicked hibernation mode.

Lampposts are so ubiquitous in even the graphitiest parts of town that no one looked at him twice as they went about their business. Lovers met under his warm light and spilled their secrets with unaccustomed honesty; businessmen swapped truths instead of fibs; gossips gossiped using disclaimers.

Not everyone, of course, wants to conduct business where other folks can see and judge him. Nindi kept a special watch out for these, as they tended to prove the most lucrative. When he spotted darting eyes and slinking steps, he made his yellow light flicker and sometimes even seem to extinguish—although in actuality, he was simply switching his light entirely over to the truth spectrum.

This sneaky behavior so appealed to the small-time crookets

and big-time crooks that they usually approached immediately and completed their purchases in full beam of his truth ray.

Oddly enough, this was the least successful of Nindi's endeavors, for the crookese, unlike the other folks, noticed the alterations in their speech patterns and passed special codes to one another, with warnings to avoid the conveniently darkening lamppost.

This was not at all what Nindi had intended, and he had to go home to his dome and think long and hard and short and soft about it. The result was an invention: the truth inverter. He mixed it in the form of ultra-thin, seemingly translucent glue, which he painted over one of his glass head plates. When he turned that plate to beam down at criminals, instead of them finding themselves forced to tell the truth out loud, the light sucked up the truth and, at Nindi's direction, stored it in a little box to be sold at auction the following week. The only sort of box that could hold a truth was one made of soul wood, which was how he first came across that marvelous material.

These auctions were Nindi's true success, and the primary source of his funding. Before long, he was making enough to build his dome and to spend more time on his hobbies.

All of Master Nindi's interests centered around light and, specifically, light's ability to affect reality (although he sometimes suspected that what he perceived as reality was in truth light, or at least would cease to exist were light snuffed out). Only light, Nindi hypothesized, could illuminate reality; the trick was simply to find the right type of light.

If there were spectrums of visible light, invisible light, and truth light, there must be other spectrums of light. He therefore went on a quest for bioluminescence. He traveled, without apparent fear for his life, into deep dark caves where glowworms nested, and he traveled into deeper, darker caves for glowrocks—which he soon found were not rocks at all but a particularly slow-moving variety of slug. Shining the power of his photokinesis on himself, he climbed perilous peaks and lassoed luminous clouds that kept their edges limned with light in skies where darkness reigned. He put advertisements in newspapers and whispered into soul boxes rumors of what he searched for, that they might be spread throughout the country.

Nindi learned much from this study, and he acquired his insect aides via much experimentation, but he did not find the light of reality as he had the light of truth. How to find it, was the question. He began with what he knew: he had often observed that different types of light came from different sources, and that the exact color (and part of a spectrum a particular color targeted) of light varied depending on *precisely* which species of fungus exuded it.

(The eggplants had been a mistake, but as he had found himself unable to get rid of them, he had gotten used to them.)

Nindi encountered soul light completely by mistake. One evening, while he was grudgingly wasting his time collecting rumors to fund his light research, a supremely ancient crone hobbled beneath his truth light. She leaned against him for support, gasping as if she could not catch her breath, and expired.

Freed, her soul beamed pure light that was not invisible or visible or truth—and rose away from her. Nindi hurriedly switched his head around to the truth-sucking side, and trapped the soul inside a soul wood box.

Breakthroughs, they say, are not made by examining the ordinary but the extraordinary. After that day, Nindi harvested souls regularly and stored them in soul boxes. He made other discoveries—that, for example, souls are most comfortably stored in places that mimic their original homes. As humanoid souls generally reside in the back, they flourish best (that is, he could harvest the most light from them) when tucked into chair backs.

In addition to being interesting, harvesting soul light was lucrative. Not that he sold it, oh, no: he used it to change reality in subtle ways, to match his desires. Unfortunately, even the best-stored souls tended to fade within a few months, and so he had to continually harvest more to keep up a constant supply, let alone increase his power.

"I must manufacture artificial soul light," he told himself. "But how? I do not know how souls produce light! I need something to compare these souls to, to discover how they work. I need a being that has a soul but that, by all rights, should not."

And so he looked.

7
The Soul Chamber

Although he never fooled himself into believing he stayed in the dome by choice, the Clockmaker found himself as happy as he had been since childhood. True, the threat of desoulization perpetually loomed, but the Clockmaker swiftly adapted to that, and it had compensations.

Whenever he was present, Master Nindi kept his assistants busy scurrying about and helping with his experiments. He exclaimed gleefully when the Clockmaker demonstrated his prowess at hand crafts, and immediately began teaching him more advanced mechanics. Soon, the Clockmaker was repairing Nindi's inventions and building new ones to his specifications.

Nature had not gifted Nindi with a personality that excelled at teaching. An ordinary student, without the precision, memory, and endless patience of clockwork, would have enraged him beyond endurance. The Clockmaker knew this, because near the beginning, Puzzle Girl joined them. She hardly lasted an hour before dissolving into tears under Master Nindi's abuse and running to the safety of their room.

"You don't want to be helping Nindi anyway," said Raskolnikov, who claimed he was ignorant at all things mechanical and that his paws weren't suited to it anyway, although he somehow never claimed this while actively under Nindi's truth light.

"But I wanted to *learn!*" Puzzle Girl wailed. "I wanted to learn something for myself and not just out of these *memories!*"

"Tell me more about your memories," Raskolnikov suggested. "Did the Warty Warlock know a great deal of magic?"

The Clockmaker, whose imagination unraveled ever more in his brain, and who had been well-trained by Raskolnikov these past months, immediately distracted the master on his favorite subject: "If the basic unit of visible light is the photon," he said, "what is the basic unit of soul light?"

Master Nindi lit up with pleasure. "The phantom, of course," he said. "Fascinating topic. Did you know that if you isolate a single photon of light, it still acts as if it's communing with other photons? As if other realities overlaid our own and could interact with our own only at the level of light! I have theorized that something similar must occur with soul light—a phantom plane touching our own. Imagine if we could tap into it—it could provide an infinite source of soul power. But there's no proof!"

His headlight flared abruptly, and he beamed the full power of his truth light upon the Clockmaker. "Do you know anything about such a plane? Could you build me a device to tap into it—or, better yet, to take me there?"

"I do not know," the Clockmaker said truthfully. "I have never before heard of such a place."

Nindi grunted in dissatisfaction but backed off. "This dome is filthy," he said. "Go sweep something."

The dome was in fact spotless nowadays, due to the Clockmaker's fastidiousness, but the Clockmaker supposed there was always more to be done.

The other compensation for being trapped in this perilous existence was, of course, the Clockmaker's new friends. Fond though he had been of The World's Greatest Poet and The World's Even Better Poet and Vialia, they had never been his equals—never worked with him on common ground, never survived with him against the same odds.

"Think about the Phantom Plane," Raskolnikov urged, when the Clockmaker told them about his conversation. "Don't tell Nindi what you're after, but learn everything you can from him—and figure out how to build a machine to the Phantom Plane."

"But I am not sure I can," the Clockmaker objected. "The Phantom Plane might not even exist!"

"Then figure out how to build a machine to take us somewhere else, and we'll tell him it's to the Phantom Plane—if it ever becomes relevant. Don't worry," he interrupted the Clockmaker's opening mouth; "we'll help you."

"What are you planning?" Puzzle Girl asked. "And don't tell me nothing, because I won't believe you."

"Nothing is exactly what I'm going to tell you," Raskolnikov retorted. "And while you're at it, Clockmaker, you need to make yourself a self-repair kit. Tell Nindi you need to use his supplies."

"I'm sure he won't find *that* suspicious!" Puzzle Girl exclaimed.

Raskolnikov stopped cleaning his face with his paws long enough to roll his eyes. "It's all in the delivery. Clockmaker, you don't like repairing yourself in the main dome because of the possibility of dust—correct? I've heard you complain about it."

"The dust does worry me," the Clockmaker admitted, "no matter how I scrub. Master Nindi always creates more."

"And it's a real hassle, carrying everything you need back to this room whenever you want to do a little touching up."

"I do not mind."

"But it *is* a hassle," Raskolnikov insisted. "And what about when Nindi is stealing souls and crafting chairs? You don't have access to the tools then."

He'd hit a sore point. The Clockmaker desperately wanted to help build the chairs, or at least learn how their admirable craftsmanship was achieved, and all of them were wild to know exactly how Master Nindi stole souls. Not even Raskolnikov, who was both small and determined, had managed to sneak in and watch; whenever Nindi set up to extract souls, he locked them in their room behind an impenetrable light barrier. No hole existed through which even a hamster could squeeze, and when the Clockmaker dutifully bored holes through the walls, ceiling, and floor at Raskolnikov's request, they found only more of the light barrier.

Despite this, Raskolnikov invariably attempted to escape being locked away and tested the barrier when he invariably *was* locked away—but to no avail.

"Someday," he would say grimly, "Nindi will slip up, and then we'll have him."

"Your hope does you credit," said Puzzle Girl.

Raskolnikov snorted. "Not hope. Conviction in fallibility."

The closest any of them had gotten to discovering Nindi's soul-extraction technique was in the various sessions Master Nindi held to search for evidence of their souls.

It happened like this: Master Nindi would summon them together into the center of the dome and turn the full power of the magnesium light upon them. This light, he claimed, augmented his natural abilities. Whenever the light was turned on them, Sharpig would go crazy for eggplants, and Raskolnikov would curl up smaller than seemed possible and mumble a mantra of swear words. The Clockmaker would cover his eyes with both hands and wait patiently. Only Puzzle Girl could look directly into the spotlight and see it and—like the eggplants—bask in it.

"It's like looking into magic," she told the Clockmaker when asked. "The Warty Warlock"—her gaze went distant, as it did when falling into his sensations—"there was a lot he didn't understand, but you only have to look into magic once to be considered a warlock, you know, and he looked in twice. He liked to boast of that, because his rival, the Pimply Warlock, had only managed it once. . . ."

Having examined them to his satisfaction, Master Nindi would pick one of them to accompany him, lock the others behind the light barrier, and head for the Soul Identification and Extraction Chamber.

And there was light.

Master Nindi's researches into the sources of natural, unnatural, semi-natural, and demi-unnatural light had not gone to waste. In addition to bioluminescence, he gave dissertations on any number of light sources—on the fission furnace sun and the thirsty moon; on lightning storms and darkening storms; on halogen, fluorescent, and neon; on high intensity and low; on magnetic and detractic light; and on tigers burning bright in the forests of the night (which last one the Clockmaker had already learned about from The World's Greatest Poet). No source of light escaped Nindi's ability to wax lyric—and yet, in the end, it was humble lyric wax that lit the Soul Chamber.

LYRIC WAX:

Rendered from the fat of butterflies caught in the extremely musical Wambrig Desert, the siren properties of lyric wax render it both inimical to most life forms and utterly irresistible. . . .

The Clockmaker listened in awe, straining his clockwork ears to identify and locate the sound. He had never heard anything like it. It was not like the music of soul wood or of the boxes Vialia had created; here were no doo-waps or tinkling waterfalls of notes. This—this—

Was this what people meant, when they called something beautiful? This sink of sadness, this well of awe, this flush of longing?

For the first time, he instinctively understood the difference between noise and music, and the sludge of Imaginarium lurched within him with the desire to compose something himself, that he might grasp this beauty and renew it again and again and again.

Master Nindi had switched his headlamp entirely to the truth spectrum, so that the only light in the chamber sang from the minuscule candle, as thin as a match and half its height, its fuchsia flame pullulating along with its melody.

As the Clockmaker's whole attention fell into the candle, Master Nindi, who was quite tone deaf, moved around him, scanning him with various spectrums of light, occasionally interrupting the music with a disgruntled grunt.

After seven minutes ten seconds—subsequent candles in later sessions never exceeded nine minutes twenty-five seconds—the music died and the fuchsia flame puffed out in an explosion of putrid smoke.

Nindi's ordinary light flared back. "You did not sleep," he observed.

The Clockmaker examined his feelings. The longing for beauty remained, but the candle's extinction did not devastate him; he suspected that Master Nindi had many more. In any case, he remembered the music flawlessly, and knew he could recreate it as soon as he learned how to make music. "I do not sleep," he said.

"Nonsense," said Master Nindi. "All living beings sleep. Even jellyfish sleep. Single-celled organisms go through stages of decreased activity. Sleep is essential for our brains to repair themselves, to decide which memories to retain and which to discard. Dreams grant us the freest expression of imagination outside of psychosis, and must be treasured as such. When else are we truly free, are our minds truly free, than in sleep?"

The Clockmaker had grown accustomed to his friends ceasing to function for long periods of time, and to the fact that this was the only way they could wind themselves up. But he did not have to like the idea of sleep or think it anything but inefficient or discuss it with Master Nindi. "Did you find my soul?" he asked.

Master Nindi's expression grew shuttered. "Not," he said, "yet."

They continued like this—the non-voluntary assistants cleaning up after Master Nindi's soul stealing in between being experimented upon themselves—until Master Nindi brought back a new maybe-soul. Her name was Gasp, and she was nearly invisible, being formed of svisteem—that substance somewhere between smoke, mist, and steam. The smoke, she told them shyly, came from incense. Myrrh, to be exact.

"I can smell that, thank you," Raskolnikov said dryly.

This comment left Gasp so offended that it took Puzzle Girl three hours of coaxing to get her to even make eye contact. When Gasp finally began to thaw, Puzzle Girl's work was nearly destroyed by the Clockmaker wondering aloud to Raskolnikov if their new friend was perhaps ill, and Raskolnikov replying that Gasp was just self-absorbed.

"Because she is svisteem, you mean," the Clockmaker said, realizing. "I have often observed that dew condenses and evaporates each morning on grass and that in winter, windows become speckled with water that the least negligence will allow to form into black mold—which my father spoke of with such horror that I am not surprised Gasp should fear it. She should speak to my good friends The World's Greatest Poet and The World's Even Better Poet. They are fluvrons, and may assist her in getting a covenant with a clever glass-a-form."

Gasp was inclined to take even greater offense at this exchange, but Puzzle Girl salvaged the situation by roundly blaming males for everything. Only then did a sniffling Gasp reveal that her mist had lain heavy over the graveyards of Traum and her steam issued from a waste reduction plant (of the herbivorous variety).

That was as much of her story as they learned before Master Nindi appeared and took her away to be examined. She was gone so long they felt sure Nindi must have found her soul and created a chair on the spot.

"Oh, no," Gasp said, giggling, when she finally returned. "We just had a nice long chat. What a pleasant lamppost he is! And how brilliant! Why, I think he must know everything there is to know!"

"Except how to find our souls," said Raskolnikov.

"Oh, I don't know about *that*," Gasp snapped, shimmering irritably—and refused to speak to any of them for the rest of that day.

In the evening, Master Nindi came for her again, and remained in conference with her all night.

"I don't like this," Raskolnikov commented, the fourth night in a row she was gone. "And I don't trust her."

"She's in the same boat as the rest of us," Puzzle Girl pointed out.

"Is she? I wonder."

The Clockmaker was equally displeased, for lack of activity and lack of access to his tools. He scrubbed their room until Raskolnikov snapped at him, whereupon he started on the eggplants against Sharpig's protestations.

"We'll play a game," Puzzle Girl offered, to settle him. "Hide-and-seek. If you hide, Raskolnikov—"

Raskolnikov shook his head. "He'll search this place top to bottom with mechanical efficiency; you know he will."

"A creative game, then. A story one sentence at a time. Oh, come on, you know he wants to improve his imagination—"

"I," said Raskolnikov, "am going to try again to get out and spy on them. I've a feeling it's desperately important we find out what they're conspiring about. You three can help me."

But there was simply no way through.

Weeks passed, Gasp retained her soul, and things seemed to return to what they had been before. Master Nindi spent his nights bringing in fresh souls and sordid gossip and struggling truths. He scanned his assistants for souls and asked them penetrating questions. He was, perhaps, sharper than before when grilling them on philosophy and soulology, but that was all.

Then one day, examining them under the magnesium light, he chose to take both Sharpig and Gasp into the Soul Chamber.

Never before had they been admitted two at a time, and Raskolnikov, the Clockmaker, and Puzzle Girl all began protesting immediately. But Master Nindi only swept them away with a barrier of light, back into their room to await the break of day.

"Don't worry," Puzzle Girl told Raskolnikov, who wouldn't stop pacing. "He'll be fine. He'll be back—"

"As a chair," Raskolnikov said. "Don't kid yourself. She's betrayed us. Sharpig is dead."

"There's no use giving up hope," Puzzle Girl insisted.

But Raskolnikov was right. When they were finally released into the main dome, they found Gasp waiting beside a freshly carved banquet table that hummed an earworm to itself, a familiar ditty composed by the famous gourmet-poet W.S. Jostlepike—

Is this a fork and knife I see before me,

And laden plates of food? Come, let me eat you;
I have you not, and yet my eyes devour.
Must I wait, with good manners, light-headed
With hunger at this?

"You fool," Raskolnikov spat at the svisteem. "You unmitigated simpleton. You've signed your own death warrant as well as ours."

Gasp sizzled with laughter. "I don't think so. He needs me too much."

Raskolnikov lunged at her, but his gnashing teeth could find no purchase on smoke or mist or steam.

The Clockmaker did not see Raskolnikov again that day. He heard Puzzle Girl calling for him, off and on, and Gasp occasionally murmuring a deprecating comment, but he ignored such distractions.

He set himself, first, to examining every inch of the banquet table; he thought he owed Sharpig that. And when he understood every joint and bevel, and the muck of Imaginarium was shooting lightning up his spine, he carefully disassembled the table into legs and top and carried the diverse pieces over to Nindi's woodshop.

Vaguely, he was aware that Gasp was screaming at him to stop and soaking his encasement with her breath. He ordered a monstrous centipede to fetch him a towel and kept going.

Of everything in the main dome, only the woodshop stood out-of-bounds. The Clockmaker had never used it or seen it used, but that didn't stop him from diving in with his usual clockwork efficiency.

Soul wood, however, proved far more difficult to maneuver than mahogany, walnut, or satinwood. Under fingers that could place a microscopic spring with utter precision, wood crumbled and snapped. The Clockmaker did not understand. He had disassembled the table without difficulty and carried the pieces over—the wood had not seemed so delicate then. What was going on?

He modified his method, used tools to hold the wood instead of his bare fingers, and wafted slivers with the wind of his hands; but no matter what he did, the soul wood disintegrated into the scattered sawdust that fed the eggplants on which Sharpig had once fed.

This was how Master Nindi found him: dusted ivory by the useless, empty remains of Nindi's first successful maybe-soul identification and removal experiment.

They had seen the lamppost angry before, but not like this.

Photokinesis punched through the maker's signature on the Clockmaker's collarbone, through the multitude of precise wheels and springs above his heart and attaching his shoulder to his body. The Clockmaker found himself flung through the air and against the far wall. He swung there, staring at the beam of solid light pinning him to the dome, twenty-five feet above the ground.

Master Nindi's headlight shone hotter and redder as he stalked forward, the intensity melting the Clockmaker's bronze and stainless steel and platinum. The fine details liquefied and ran down his chest like rain.

"Stop!" Puzzle Girl cried. "Stop it!" She threw herself at Nindi, but one tentacle batted her contemptuously away. She clattered to the floor in a pile of broomsticks and flatware, but she sprang up again a moment later. Her eyes shone as they shone when she gazed into the magnesium light.

Puzzle Girl tore a daisy up by the roots and hurled it at Nindi. Midair, the daisy stretched and uncurled. Its stem whipped around like a scorpion tail, catching Nindi's pole and latching on. The hyena head, twice as large as before, ripped razor teeth into living metal.

Nindi screamed, and the Clockmaker crashed to the ground.

He had not been built to fall; he weighed far too much. He was aware of . . . shattering.

I shall have to rebuild my legs, he thought, dazed.

"I said *stop it!*" Puzzle Girl ordered. "It wasn't his fault—*I* told him to do it, you evil *flashlight* of a lamppost! You deserve to be *extinguished!*"

The Clockmaker raised his head with considerable difficulty. Acid green gas swirled around Puzzle Girl's outstretched arms and planted feet, and her eyes shone bright as two stars.

"Can you move?" Raskolnikov asked urgently.

The Clockmaker tilted his head. The hamster had popped up by his side, jittering with adrenaline. "My legs are broken," he said dumbly. "And my shoulder—"

"I have eyes!" Raskolnikov snapped. "I asked if you could move."

The Clockmaker considered. "I could pull myself along," he conceded. "Why?"

"Because," Raskolnikov said grimly, "Puzzle Girl is going to lose—and we need to be out of sight when she does. Her sacrifice isn't going to do us any good otherwise."

The Clockmaker did not see Master Nindi again until the next night. He and Raskolnikov had spent the entire preceding day locked in their room behind the light barrier, and they hadn't wasted a moment of it. Gravely gleeful, viciously victorious, Raskolnikov interrogated the Clockmaker on everything he had done and told him exactly what he was to do next.

The Clockmaker waited motionless for Master Nindi from the instant the sun set. When Master Nindi cast aside the light barrier and swept in, the Clockmaker immediately demanded, "How can I make a Phantom Plane Transporter for you if you are going to break me whenever I begin?"

Nindi, who had fully intended to take the Clockmaker away to be desouled at once, paused. "What are you talking about?"

"Inspiration struck me like lightning," the Clockmaker said. "That table was the key to creating a transporter. I almost had it—I was sure I had—but the soul wood kept breaking! And then you attacked me!"

Nindi's light narrowed suspiciously. "Don't give me that. Everyone knows that soul wood can only be worked under the soothing influence of lyric wax light."

"I did not know," the Clockmaker said.

Master Nindi switched his spectrum to full truth light, but he

93

needn't have bothered; the Clockmaker had not lied. Inspiration—wild, desperate, grieving inspiration—had shocked through him as he had examined Sharpig's table. Not inspiration out of nowhere; he had for many weeks, at Raskolnikov's behest, been considering the Phantom Plane and asking Nindi questions about it. Anguish had simply boiled down his knowledge into the pot of imagination and produced inspiration within his gut.

"Tell me the truth," ordered Master Nindi: "can you build me a Phantom Plane Transporter?"

"I need Raskolnikov," the Clockmaker said, "and I need to be fully repaired. Unfortunately, I also need Sharpig's table—and, through my own ignorance, through lack of instruction regarding the working of soul wood, it is no more."

"Don't worry about *that,*" said Nindi. "I have a replacement."

"One untouched, undamaged? One whose soul light has not been siphoned off to fuel your reality experiments?"

"As you must have guessed. And," said Nindi, "if *she* does not work, I have another."

"I need Raskolnikov."

"I was not speaking of him."

"I am glad to hear it," said the Clockmaker. "There is one thing more. You have damaged me unjustly and owe me reparation. I want a portable repair kit of my own before I begin on the transporter. And once I do begin, I require access to any tools and materials I request."

Nindi laughed. "Build me my transporter," he said, "and you can have anything your heart of crystal desires." He turned and swept through the room, to gather rumors and truths and, perhaps, to make some adjustments to the system Gasp had helped him build so that she would no longer be necessary.

"Well done," Raskolnikov murmured in the Clockmaker's ear. "Very well done."

8

The Phantom Plane

Nowhere in the multiverse lives a race of people as abominably dishonest as the Forsoothians. Crab-legged, blue-snouted, thirty-fingered beings, the Forsoothians' most infamous trait is their inability to speak anything but the exact truth. This gives them such a fearsome reputation as conmen, business sharks, attorneys, and (unjustly) liars, that the country of Forsooth has no government, though it is startlingly wealthy. This is because 100% of goods and money exchanged are exchanged on the black market. Since black markets legally do not exist and therefore cannot be taxed, governments cannot thrive without tax money, and nothing can be legally declared to exist without a government, Forsooth does not exist.

When asked where they are from, therefore, Forsoothians can truthfully say "nowhere"; when asked whether they are from Forsooth, they reply "no"—for no such place exists. After all, what is truth but that which is accepted as true? What is truth but that which is in accordance to fact and reality? Perhaps if reality were less utterly malleable or less blatantly open to interpretation, even tens of hundreds of generations of Forsoothians could not have sunk into their bog of deception, but I doubt it.

Unlike the Forsoothians, the Clockmaker preferred to be not only truthful but also honest—which is why, when he was working so diligently on Master Nindi's Phantom Plane Transporter, he did not ask Raskolnikov what he was up to, and he averted his eyes whenever he feared he might see too much. For though if asked, under the truth light, whether Raskolnikov had any mechanical skill, he could truthfully say that the hamster had invariably maintained he *hadn't*, this answer would have been dishonest, and so he'd rather avoid it if he could.

Master Nindi left them alone as they worked. And, as Master Nindi must have guessed would happen, the Clockmaker timed his completion of the teleportation device to the daylight hours, when Nindi was asleep. There was absolutely nothing to stop the Clock-maker from scooping Raskolnikov onto his shoulder, picking up the thousand-piece puzzle—the teleportation controller—that was all that remained of their friend, and activating the device.

Light flashed, compressed, encompassed . . . and they arrived.

Though he had not expressed it in such words, even to himself, the Clockmaker's imagination had been working on what the Phantom Plane must look like. It must first, he thought, be brightly lit—maybe not solid light, but with flashes as searingly bright as the magnesium light. Amorphous forms would be floating about, tinged slightly coral; these would be the souls. He would be able to hear them as through many layers of cloth, speaking to him. Puzzle Girl's voice would call to him amidst the throng, clearer than the rest, and lead him—

Here, his imagination had splintered into many paths, each fading away into the fogs of possibility and awaiting solid information.

What he actually found was . . . not as expected. There *was* light, but it glowed thick and orange-red through a nearly opaque sky. The sky looked closer than usual too, but the Clockmaker didn't trust his distance perception enough to be sure.

Then there was the ground or floor or—standing surface. Rather squashy yellowish white, and simultaneously sticky and slick. The Clockmaker was reminded faintly of the dough he'd manipulated in Creation's bakery, in Imaginarium. Certainly, there was something foodish about it. His feet imprinted ankle deep in its surface, which slowly oozed upward.

"Free," Raskolnikov murmured. "After so long."

Not for the first time, the Clockmaker wondered how many years Raskolnikov had been trapped in the dome. "I am afraid Master Nindi must have guessed what we would do and planned for it," he said apologetically. "As soon as he is awake, he will harvest Gasp's soul and follow us."

"Oh," breathed Raskolnikov, "I'm counting on it."

The Clockmaker smiled slightly. "You altered the device. I thought you had, though you said you did not know anything about mechanics."

"I *don't* know anything about mechanics," Raskolnikov rejoined. "Explosives, now . . ." He trailed off into happy thoughts.

The Clockmaker soon had other things on his mind. Small cracks were forming outward from him, and he recognized the stress pattern from a stepped-on clock face he'd once replaced. "I believe," the Clockmaker said, "that my weight is excessive for the surface tension of this ground."

Raskolnikov sent him an amused glance. "You really *have* no sense of smell," he said. "No one else could fail to recognize Stinking Limffort."

"Stinking Limffort!" exclaimed the Clockmaker. "Stinking Limffort as in,

> "tangy
> molded
>   raw emotion cooked
> cooked cheese raw
>   taste explosion"

"and,

> "All that's stinky is not cheese;
> Often have I been displeased.
> Many a Brie has been a tease—
> But Limffort always is my wheeze.

"—*That* Stinking Limffort?"

"The very same," Raskolnikov confirmed.

"Then all of Master Nindi's theories were wrong," the Clockmaker concluded, shaking his head in amazement. "Reality-changing light comes not from souls but from cheese. Poor Puzzle Girl! If only we had known."

For some reason, this made Raskolnikov laugh and keep laughing and nearly fall off the Clockmaker's shoulder in hysterics.

The Clockmaker waited patiently for the paroxysm to die down and Raskolnikov to elucidate. It took some time, and Raskolnikov still squeaked and jittered as he cried, "We're not in the Phantom Plane! While I was rigging your transporter, I changed the location."

"But—why?" the Clockmaker asked, slightly hurt to have his invention altered without his knowing.

"Because I don't want to go there—and neither should you. How would we survive? There might not be air—or gravity—or food! And how would we get back?"

The Clockmaker gazed at him, halfway between admiration at his inference and annoyance at his interference. "Then where are we?"

"How should I know?" Raskolnikov asked. "I've never been here before. A giant cheese on a giant's dinner plate, maybe. I vote we leave as quickly as possible."

Not the Phantom Plane After All, Apparently

The Clockmaker was free. The Clockmaker had friends with him. The Clockmaker had purpose. "I will build Puzzle Girl a new body," he proclaimed to Raskolnikov as they tromped across the surface of the cheese—or, rather, as the Clockmaker tromped and Raskolnikov clung on to the ridges of his shoulder. The shoulder had not been built to be clung on to, as Raskolnikov pointed out more than once. The Clockmaker had offered to carry him in his hands, but Raskolnikov had replied more acerbically than strictly necessary that he would not be so degraded. "I will build a body for her soul to live in," the Clockmaker clarified, "and she will be a living work of art."

"You'll make the body in your own image, I suppose," Raskolnikov said.

The Clockmaker's wheels clicked softly as he thought. "I have found," he said slowly, "my own body most satisfactorily made. I conclude, however, that you would disapprove of giving Puzzle Girl such a body—and I have a feeling that you would be right to disapprove, although I am not sure why."

"Then I've done some good," Raskolnikov said. "Don't worry; I'll stick around to make sure you don't bungle it. I owe Puzzle Girl *that.*"

The Clockmaker circumnavigated a rather gooey spot, the cheese sucking on his metal feet. The further they went, the less set the cheese became. The Clockmaker finally stopped and turned around, only to find that the cheese had sprung back over his footprints and that every direction looked the same. His memory could, of course, have taken him back blindfolded, but he did not trust the cheese not to have shifted in his absence.

"Don't go wandering," Raskolnikov advised. "Keep in a straight line, and we'll hit something eventually. So once you make this body for Puzzle Girl, how do you plan to get her soul into it?"

The Clockmaker held up the transporter's control. Mindful of the uncertainty of their journey, he had secured the puzzle inside a sheath of waterproof plastic. "I will incorporate the pieces through-out her body."

"And that will work, will it?"

"You disagree."

Raskolnikov shrugged. "What do *I* know about magic?"

"I am not sure," the Clockmaker said. "You seem to know a great deal about a great number of things."

The melted pots of cheese spread further across the ground, hissing and spitting acidically. The Clockmaker found his way ever harder; he often had to stretch his legs to their full stride to step from one patch of safety to another. He made again to turn back, more seri-ously this time, only to find that his footsteps had not sprung back; they had turned into sizzling wells. There was also a feeling in the air, one so familiar he found himself aching for his home, for the little shop in Perpetua he had not seen in decades.

"Someone," he said, "is manipulating time."

"What are you talking about?"

"Can you not feel it? Time is more solid here, more pliable. Yet this has not the feel of Perpetua; someone has injected time into the cheese, or perhaps the cheese itself produces it. That is what is causing such rapid changes; they are not rapid but time-distorted."

"Lazy," Raskolnikov ground out, "not letting the cheese ripen in its own time."

His tone struck the Clockmaker as odd. The hamster's eyes bulged, rimmed white. "Allow me to carry you in my hands," the Clockmaker said. "Then I can move more quickly without dislodg-ing you."

"Fine," Raskolnikov said, and the Clockmaker knew that he was frightened indeed.

The Clockmaker tucked the puzzle securely under one arm and cupped the hamster inside both hands, with only slight slivering gaps through which Raskolnikov could peek and breathe. Then he blurred into action, whipping his feet out of the sucking cheese and toward the distant waxy edge.

The lips of a lake gasped open before them, and the Clockmaker had to spin and slide away to avoid pitching in. The puzzle went flying from under his arm—and into the lake of cheese. It landed flat on the surface, which burped and lifted. Not quickly, but unstoppably, the puzzle angled, tipped, and oozed seamlessly beneath the surface.

"What is it?" Raskolnikov cried, scrabbling to press his eyes against a gap. "What's happened?"

"The puzzle!" The Clockmaker stared after it, frozen in horror and despair. "Puzzle Girl!" If he tried to edge around—

"Leave it," Raskolnikov ordered. "It's lost. Clockmaker, *leave it*, or we'll be lost too!"

"It was an accident! I could not catch it!"

"You're right: you couldn't. And you can't save her, but you can save us. We need to get moving!"

"Yes," whispered the Clockmaker. "Yes, I—yes."

There was a silence, punctuated by the crackle and pop of bubbles. The Clockmaker did not move.

"Clockmaker!" Raskolnikov shouted.

With terrible calm, the Clockmaker replied, "I appear to be stuck."

"What?"

Raskolnikov struggled until the Clockmaker got the hint and parted his hands enough for the hamster to pop his head out and look down. Hot air sliced through his fur, and the taste of sharp cheese filled his mouth.

Spikes of cyan and ming mold jolted upright out of their cheese bed, only to either settle languidly back down or thrust yet further up, blowing gusts of gas out their gaskets. Bubbles coagulated and melted, formed and bloated, belched and burst their grenade payload of fleshy fragments. Cheese pots swirled and stirred, their skirling surfaces twining yellow with white until mold tendrils wrapped through them and they solidified once more. Cheesy gas billowed thick under the red wax sky, through the tinted air, exulting in the tumult around it, the slaughter beneath it.

For here was no ordinary Stinking Limffort. Here was the Mother of All Cheeses.

8"

The Mother of All Cheeses,
Which Is Definitely Not in the Phantom Plane

CHEESE:

Unlike milk-based products such as butter and yogurt, cheese (caseus) is a genus of the mold family. When first discovered, approximately $10544(\pi)^2$ fortnights ago, cheese was the blue-green color of its closest mold relative, penicillin. Since then, cheese has increasingly evolved into the shapes, sizes, and colors most appetizing to sentient life forms.

For centuries, cheeseotonists could find no explanation for this mutation. However, in recent decades, most prestigious cheeseotonists have come to agree with Dr. I. O. Gram's explanation:

> Hosts with superior intelligence are essential
> for cheese protection and reproduction. Once
> ingested, cheese forms colonies in the sentient
> brain. From there, it can prompt the brain to
> both a) protect the cheese using rodent- and
> waterproof containers and b) eat more cheeses
> of various varieties, thus increasing the genet-
> ic diversity of the cheese breeding pool.

In this way, cheeseotonists around the world have demonstrated the practice of extremely intelligent

people being extremely thick—for, of course, all cheeses are a single organism whose disparate parts form a
hive mind. The queen and originator of all cheeses is
that great time-manipulating matriarch, the Mother
of All Cheeses.

"I cannot free myself," the Clockmaker said, "but you are not
trapped. Yonder is an island that looks solid; I could toss you there."

"Sure you could," said Raskolnikov. "And then what? Either it
turns into mush under my feet and I drown or it doesn't and I die of
thirst. No *thank* you."

This struck the Clockmaker as excellent logic. He tried again.
"I may not be able to move my legs," he said, "but I am very strong. I
could throw you a long way—perhaps beyond this time zone. Or
perhaps to the ceiling. You could cling there until things are settled."

"I could break every bone in my body, you mean. Try your legs
again. It's only cheese; you should be able to get free."

"Yes, but I cannot bend my knees," the
Clockmaker said apologetically. The
molten cheese slurped around his
thighs. "I do not understand it either; I
suspect the cheese is holding me here
on purpose."

"So that's it then," Raskolnikov
concluded. "This is it. We are going
to die. And just after escaping! Or I
will die and you will live in cheese
until it liquefies enough for you to
escape or someone eats around
you, if that ever happens."

"I do not think I will be able
to escape," the Clockmaker reflected. "For if it immobilizes me, I shall
not be able to wind myself up."

"Then we're both doomed," Raskolnikov sighed. "I should have known it would come to this."

Cheese plooped and slooped and gooped, slurping the Clock-maker in until it sucked at his hips.

The Clockmaker looked at it, looked at the hamster, and came to a decision. He opened his mouth and cried, "Help! Help!"

"What in the stinky cheese do you think you're doing?" Raskolnikov demanded.

"Calling for help. Help! Help!"

"Yes, I can hear that. But there's no one around to help us!"

"Maybe not," the Clockmaker admitted. "And if it comes to that, I will throw you to safety with the last movement of my arm. But there is always a chance. Help! Help! Help! Help! Help!"

"Ridiculous," Raskolnikov grumbled.

"Help! Help!"

The clugging, slugging cheese clugged and slugged and chugged and shrugged over the Clockmaker's belly, across his chest, and up to his chin. "HELP!" he shouted one last time, then shut his mouth firmly as the cheese crept over it.

Throughout, he held Raskolnikov in one hand, arm fully extended upward. The hamster alternately shrank and bristled at the molten cheese, shivering hard despite the heat. The Clock-maker's eyes, barely above the cheesy surface, turned to meet his. A few more inches, and Raskolnikov knew he'd be thrown, and he shivered harder to know it.

"This is stupid," Raskolnikov told the Clockmaker. "Oh, for pity's—fine! I'll do it. HELP! SOMEBODY HELP US!!"

The Clockmaker's eyes disappeared and then his brow. He cranked his arm back at the elbow.

"HELP!" Raskolnikov screamed, but the Clockmaker could no longer hear him; cheese blotted his ears as it did his eyes. He could feel nothing except cheese and Raskolnikov hunkered on his palm. He was relying on his memory for which way to throw the hamster; he had *thought* one direction looked slightly more promising than the others. He stiffened his wrist in preparation—and found himself frozen in that pose as an invisible force drew him up out of the goopy cheese and into the air. Some cheese glops glopped down, but many more clung desperately to him.

"Good grief," said a voice, familiar even through the cheese coating. "A cybernetic cheeseman. What will people think of next?"

"Are you blind?" Raskolnikov scathed, too frightened to moderate his tone. "He's only covered in cheese. Clean him off, and you'll see."

"A novel approach to curing blindness, but I'll try it."

In an instant, the cheese coating the Clockmaker slid off as if he had been suddenly coated in castor oil. He found himself face-to-face with none other than Vamazz the Vamazing.

Though his sapphire hair remained as bouffant and beautiful as ever, the rest of Vamazz looked distinctly battered: his bulky armor was charred and, in places, burned through; a cut that had only just stopped bleeding bisected one arched brow; the chains dangling from his pauldrons had been torn short and dangled loose from his waist. His magnificent, triangular hat had disappeared entirely, and the small flames that had clung to it and to the chains instead encircled his wrists. Unidentifiable stains marred his robes, and a guarded hint of pain lurked behind his brilliant eyes and in the lines that had not before wrinkled the smooth skin of his face.

"You know," said Vamazz, "I think he's the one whose blindness has been cured; Stinking Limffort is no friend to the oculars. Have an ironing board"—he spun one out of midair to match the one upon which he sat: floral and lavender—"and tell me how you ended up on the Mother of All Cheeses during time breeding. You would have been in real trouble, if I hadn't randomly happened by. Say, have we met before?"

"Yes," said the Clockmaker, "on two previous—"

"Not you," Vamazz interrupted gently; "your friend. Raskolnikov, isn't it?"

A few months' interlude had done nothing to diminish Vamazz's listening proficiency. He oohed and ahhed in amazement at descriptions of the dome, chuckled in admiration at the advance in light knowledge, and clucked his tongue disapprovingly at Master Nindi's reprehensible wickedness.

"I would have liked to see it for myself," he said. "I've been searching for a teleportation path to the dome while you talked, as I assumed you wished to return. Unfortunately, it seems the dome no longer exists. I hope you're not too disappointed."

Raskolnikov snorted, and the Clockmaker assured him they were not disappointed before detailing the arrival of Gasp and subsequent death of Sharpig. Vamazz shed a tear at this. He clutched his hands at their daring escape and exclaimed in horror when the Clockmaker pointed out the place where the puzzle had slid beneath the surface.

"Surely, sir," the Clockmaker said hopefully, "you can use your wizardry to find and rescue the puzzle—even as you rescued us."

Vamazz shook his head sadly. "If only I could. Perhaps if I had arrived sooner—but the puzzle is no longer there."

"What do you mean?" Raskolnikov demanded.

Vamazz regarded him with mild astonishment. "I should think *you* would know. My dear Raskolnikov, you lost the puzzle. It has therefore gone where all lost things go."

Raskolnikov groaned. "To the Land of the Purple Ring."

"Naturally."

The Clockmaker didn't understand why his friend looked so broken. Surely, Vamazz the Vamazing could send them to the Land of the Purple Ring as easily as—

"Hold on right there," Vamazz told him, though the Clockmaker had not said anything. "I can NOT send you to the Land of the Purple Ring; I never lose anything. But . . ." His brows creased pensively. "Perhaps . . . yes. That might work." He intertwined his fingers, wriggled his nose, and proclaimed: "Pylut! Fwingit! Blongy! Vamazz!"

9

At Sea

Satisfied with his good deed, Vamazz turned back to the reason he'd come to the Mother of All Cheeses: his supper. It had been a long day and not a painless one, and he felt he deserved a special treat. What could he prefer, thought his turquoise mind, to the queen of Stinking Limffort?

MEN WITH TURQUOISE MINDS:
Although particularly—

"You don't listen, do you?" said Vamazz the Vamazing, mid cheese scoop.

—obnoxious when it comes to things they clearly don't understand—

"I don't want you talking about this. Do I have to come up there myself?"

—such as the purpose and benefit of strong and clear narrative exposition—

"Oh, I understand all right. What I *don't* understand is why you feel you have the right to give away other people's personal information!"

—that wouldn't even bother them if they kept their eyes on their own business.

"Look," said Vamazz the Vamazing, grinding his teeth and planting his hands on his hips, "I don't want to argue about this, so I'll make a bargain with you. You stop harping on about men with turquoise minds, and I'll owe you a favor."

Vamazz clearly thought this an excellent deal, and to be fair, no sentient being in its right, left, or central cranial lobe would turn down an offer from a man with a turquoise—that is to say, from someone as illustrious as the mysterious, mystical, mayhemically magical majestic magus Vamazz the Vamazing. Knowing this, Vamazz waited only a count of four mega mcseconds before spitting on the ground to seal the deal.

Since in this case the ground was highly acidic cheese lava, the sapphire spit (for warlocks, like witches, have blue saliva they can use as ink) histled and fishnled and created that phenomenon ever after known as vectacular cheese.

VECTACULAR CHEESE:

A diamond-shaped cheese with exactly two 1/3-inch sapphire circles of mold running through each block, vectacular's hard, fuzzy white rind protects a gooey center the consistency of room-temperature cream cheese.

The cheese bears only a mildly nutty scent, and its flavor bypasses the taste buds entirely and goes straight to the brain. There, it can have a variety of effects, based on both the predisposition of the eater and other, often seemingly random factors. In one being, it might spark a sudden capacity for magic; in another, it might drive the eater mad. It can unlock brilliance or infuse a deep love of soft-boiled eggs, tribal drum music, or clashing fashion accessories. It can inspire acts of brash heroism or turn brash heroes into brutish hunks.

Professional cheeseotonists who prefer not to get sued recommend no one except those with nothing to lose ever taste vectacular, which doesn't stop said cheeseotonists gobbling it down by the fistful. Psychiatrists have successfully used it to cure suicidal depression, extreme trauma, and perpetual insomnia. Vectacular has raised children from comas, haired hairless puppies, and so far reversed memory loss as to induce hallucination.

For all the good it has done, however, over the span of eternity, vectacular will have done far more harm: for (although the general public has no absolute proof of this) vectacular was what turned Ivan the Mild into that most destructive, detrimental, demonic assault on all civilized senses to influence radio play in over 1000.4 years—Ivan the Rock Star.

Chuckling rather, Vamazz the Vamazing tucked his slice of cheese inside his armor, scooped his hands toward his own body, proclaimed: "Phalta! Ghoolash! Futavore! Vamazz!" and vanished with a puff of turquoise and a faint smell of salmon.

He landed in a small, ratty town at the base of a hill—or what had been a hill; it was mostly now a smoky caldera littered with ashy remnants and small fires. Several villagers gasped when he appeared, but he ignored them in favor of striding forward and up. He appeared to look neither left nor right, but in truth he carefully noted the conspicuous absence of lampposts and the roughly gaping holes where they'd been recently ripped out of concrete, asphalt, and earth. He would, he thought, have to look into that.

Vamazz had been quite interested to see the dome and meet

Master Nindi, who struck him as an odd sort of lamppost and an odder sort of scientist: an expert in souls who was apparently blind to the fact that Raskolnikov had stored his in a phylactery. Based on the glowing signature this storage had left behind, Vamazz guessed it had been performed during a stint with the wizard Galapagos.

"We don't talk about *that one*," Vamazz muttered sharply.

Equally odd was Nindi's uncertainty about the Clockmaker, whose soul was so obviously indistinguishable from his heart of crystal that a child could have seen it. And yet Nindi could not have been wholly incompetent, if he had elsewhere succeeded so consistently!

Although Vamazz longed to meet this contradictory lamppost, one look at the wreckage assured him that none could have survived the explosion. The only things that *had* survived were a number of chair backs that had been crafted using the most agonizingly fragile wood in existence.

That these chair backs had survived struck Vamazz as an unpleasantly incomplete and unbalanced state of affairs, and so he immediately set about rectifying the situation: he wriggled his fingers and flicked his nose and murmured various mystical words.

With a contented chorus, the chair backs subsided into sawdust, and their captives breathed free.

The Clockmaker landed in a cloud of shrimp, their veins pulsing with liquid gold that glimmered and shifted in a way cheese never could. They floated around him, croaking and oohing, bumping into his forehead and sliding along his chest. The Clockmaker waved them away, which is how he realized that both of his hands were empty.

"Raskolnikov?" His voice sounded hollow and pleading as it bounced off squishy flying shrimp and back to his ears. "Raskolnikov, where are you?"

"Ras!" the shrimp parroted back at him. "Kol! Ni! Kov!" Their whiskers fluttered as they flew, spiraling outward in shifting fractals, glimmering gold in the sconce-light. "Ni! Nik! Ov! Ik!"

Perhaps, the Clockmaker thought, he simply could not hear the hamster over the cries of the shrimp, simply could not see him past their uselessly dangling legs and bloated C-shaped bodies. But the hamster had a way of being heard, when he wanted to be, and he had no reason to hide.

Something lurched in the Clockmaker's chest, sending him off balance. He had never felt the fatigue that prompted fleshy beings to sit down, but he had often observed that when upset, his father and Vialia would plop themselves tiredly down and press their foreheads into their hands.

Between pulsing gold veins and pumpkin-and-white flesh, he caught a glimpse of a chair—no, a throne! One sturdy enough to support 583 pounds of clockwork man. So the Clockmaker sat and pressed his forehead in his palm and tried to feel better.

He did not feel better. He felt worse, as if something were trying to claw through his chest. With an imagination he had once not possessed, he reflected on how strange it was that a heart made of the hardest substance in the world could be so tender.

In his unhappiness, the Clockmaker hardly noticed the shrimp floating away until they were suddenly gone—clearing the air so he could return the gazes of the skeleton crew that had stopped work to watch him with gouged-out eye sockets. Fragments of desiccated skin hung about their hips as loincloths, and one or two retained a few wisps of hair, but otherwise the sun had bleached their bones bone-white, and insects had picked them clean. Ragged teeth bared in grinning skulls, and knobbly fingers curled and uncurled around ropes, axes, staves, and other accoutrements of murder.

The Clockmaker stood quickly, and felt the chair squelch beneath him. Mildly alarmed, he flicked on higher magnification and took a look.

The throne had been constructed entirely out of shrimp. Living micro-miniature shrimp, smaller cousins of those flying around, their bodies crushed together so compactly that he could barely see where one ended and another began. The crushing made their veins and eyes bulge, so that the throne seemed to be pulsing with swirling gold like oil on water and interspersed with black bulbs. The crafter had arranged the shrimp in spirals, and patterned the throne itself on its material: its wings and arm rests ended in curls like shrimp tails.

The Clockmaker had an alarming thought and hurriedly checked his backside, but he found it blessedly clean: unscraped, unsmeared, unmarred by shrimp guts. What a risk he had taken, sitting down!

The skeleton crew stepped forward, and the Clockmaker snapped his attention back up to them. They stepped again, in time and with perfect synchronization. As the Clockmaker opened his mouth to try to explain, they fell into tight dance choreography, singing:

> When he stands aloft in his bird nest,
>> Under the grin of the flag he flies,
> He knows no ship in the fleet can best
>> His guns; and any that tries, then dies.

> Away from the sea and the land he knew,
>> Sailing with only a skeleton crew,
> He went too far and the sun him fried,
>> But he lived and died
>>> A pirate king.

> Hip-hip! Beware of the pirate king,
> Beware of the clockwork king.

The crew threw themselves forward, to freeze in a pleading dance pose, arms outstretched toward the Clockmaker.

The Clockmaker looked wildly back and forth. It was clear to him that he should respond in kind, but he didn't know any appropriate songs. He didn't think the folksongs his father had taught him would be fitting, as they were all about nurseries and wolves and cannibalistic witches and never mentioned piratical adventures once. True, he had thought about composing his own tunes, but he hadn't had the chance. And the only other tunes he knew—

The sailors were growing impatient, their eyes narrowing and their weapons rising. So the Clockmaker opened his mouth and activated not his voice, but the chimes his father had installed in case he ever wanted to toll the hour . . . and he sang the music of the lyric wax.

This was not what the skeleton crew had expected or requested or known existed, and the Clockmaker did not dance in accompaniment because he had not been designed to dance. Not being traditionally alive, and the Clockmaker's rendition not having the unmitigated power of wax, the skeleton crew fell neither into stupor nor into sleep; but after a minute, they joined their voices to his, and they swayed along.

As captain and pirate king, the Clockmaker's first act (after acquiring a suitably giant pirate king hat with a fluffy feather, as every king must have to consolidate his power) was to state their new mission:

"We will stop at every harbor, every island," he announced, "until we find the Land of the Purple Ring."

Unless it is landlocked, he thought, and wished Raskolnikov were there. He swore to himself that he would find the hamster too, one day. In the meantime, he had better dive into learning everything there was to know about sailing the ocean blue.

The other pirates took the Clockmaker under their skeletal wings with a will, especially the boatswain—an enormously tall, narrow fellow named Sullivan. He led the Clockmaker through the general management of the ship, and ordered the lower ranks to teach him their trades. From the sailing master, the Clockmaker learned to read maps and stars, to chart courses and steer the ship. From the powder monkey and gunners, he learned how to clean, operate, and aim the cannons, although he did not learn to be comfortable with the idea of damaging other ships. From the swabbies, he learned piratical moping techniques, which he rejected utterly in favor of what his father had taught him. From that day forth, the captain did most of the actual cleaning on deck, because he did not trust any of his inferiors to properly scrub every cranny, crook, and corner.

"You should let your crew do the menial work," Sullivan advised him. "They won't respect you otherwise."

"Maybe," the Clockmaker agreed—but he was more concerned with cleanliness than with respect.

In addition to becoming a fine sailor in his own right, the Clockmaker learned about how the world was stuck together. Previously, most of his going between countries—arguably all of it—had been by some form of magical transportation. He had had a vague idea that most countries were physically connected, but had never before seen it for himself; only now did he begin to understand geography in its practical form and connect it to maps.

From his new vantage as captain, with Sullivan to point out and name landmasses, the Clockmaker reorganized how he saw the world. He reorganized again when he discovered that telescopes could compensate for his near-sightedness and show him what he had never before guessed: the existence of distant mountains and trees and people. How detailed they were, and in what curious clumps they arranged themselves. What light, what shadow, what clear lines and lined clarity! He had always supposed distant objects were by their nature fuzzy and undetailed and possibly nonexistent until they got close.

With his crew, the Clockmaker stepped ashore long-abandoned beaches and rowed to sprawling harbors. He learned dozens of languages, visited twenty different clockwork shops (despite the efficiency of his gyroscopic tourbillon, onboard was not ideal for delicate repairs). He remained mindful of his father's advice, but it never came into play; the moment any clockmakers saw the pirate king marching purposefully their way, easily identifiable in his fearsome feathered hat, they fled.

This fleeing disconcerted the Clockmaker at first, but he soon not only got used to it, but began to perceive it as his due. He was learning more than ship craft from the pirates: he was learning that it is a lot easier to take the treasure and use the tools of people when you don't have to fight them for the privilege.

The pirates taught him one other thing, the most important element of piratical activity: big musical numbers. He never could learn to dance, unfortunately, but his precise memory picked up every air, and he could sing *Yo ho* with the best of them. To compensate for not dancing, he provided percussion by clapping or stamping or chiming.

After about a year, Sullivan approached him as he stood at the wheel. "Captain! We have searched every coastline, every harbor, every island in this sea for the Land of the Purple Ring—save one. That one. Unfortunately, the men are superstitious about that island, and I fear that insisting they go aground will cause a mutiny. But I am faithful to you—and if you wish, I will row you out."

The Clockmaker did wish, and said so in his most pompous pirate king manner. He put his finest hat upon his head and, as the crew watched with apprehensive eye sockets, climbed into the waiting dinghy.

The current surrounding the island hardly existed, which was strange enough; but stranger still was the island itself. Not only was it completely barren of vegetation of any sort, or indeed anything save rough brown rocks, it was also startlingly cold: far colder than the pirate ship waiting not far away—like standing in the shadow of a glacier.

"What is this place? Surely not the Land of the Purple Ring," the Clockmaker said to Sullivan—only to discover that his boatswain was back in the dinghy, rowing away. "Sullivan! I have not given you permission to leave."

"I'm sorry, captain," Sullivan called back, his voice icy clear over the calm water, "but you aren't a proper pirate king—us pirates weren't meant to be explorers, and we haven't seen head nor tail nor hide nor hair nor rabbit of this land of yours. We took a vote, see, and you're out."

"This is mutiny!" the Clockmaker exclaimed.

"That's what happens to captains who don't come up to standard. But I'm sorry about the marooning, I really am, because I like you despite your deficiencies. So I'll give you a piece of advice: get off this island before night falls. The temperature will drop to absolute zero when it does, and I don't think even you could survive that." He started rowing harder, taking him out of range. At the last moment, he yelled, "Good luck!" and then he was nearly back to the ship, which sailed away the moment it had its boatswain aboard.

The Clockmaker stared after the departing ship. He had had no idea his crew had thought so little of him. Rackstraw, Frederic, Pointdex—was he nothing to any of them? Worse than nothing, that they not only could not wait to get rid of him but left him here, where he was sure to die?

Escape before nightfall. Four hours, twelve minutes, fifty-six seconds from now. But what escape was there?

The Clockmaker turned his attention to the island.

Blue-gray shards of stone jutted up at mad angles, exploding in giant lily formations—the closest things to life this island had to offer. It was the sort of stone that would look just the same under ice, worn to smooth slivers by the salty wind. The Clockmaker touched a shard, but it was stronger than it looked, and did not break in his hand until he applied bone-shattering pressure.

The island was very small. The Clockmaker walked around it, slowly and searchingly, in eleven minutes. He found many more lily flower explosions of stone, and nothing else. No rough raft awaited him; no seam indicated a trap door or cave. There weren't even bones left.

The Clockmaker could not fly and he could not swim; his only way off the island was to walk. He was waterproof to thirty fathoms, and he knew full well that the numbers clockmakers put on their pieces were generally far below their actual waterproofing. But he also knew the sea was deep, and that the closest land—to the west—lay more than eighty miles distant.

Obedient to Sullivan's suggestion, the Clockmaker shut his ears and mouth and walked west into the water.

Wet cold replaced dry cold, and water covered his vision. It did *not* feel like wading in the hungry water in the depths of the Tomb of Ego the Maniac. It pressed on him, and its torrent tugged him this way and that. Silvery fish flashed.

The influence of the island stretched far beyond its borders. The moving water wasn't so bad, the further out he got, but the sandy stone beneath his feet blistered with cold and, he suspected, would freeze the water solid not long after nightfall.

The Clockmaker walked further out, keeping a careful calculation of the angle of his feet and the depth of the water. The land around the water sloped down very quickly, after the initial plateau. He stopped when he reached thirty fathoms, and looked around. The afternoon sunlight penetrated enough that he could see, although the water below him dimmed to bare twilight. Dark silhouettes swam lazily above him, uninterested in something that neither smelled nor acted like food. Only kurisharks were unwise enough to chomp a metal man.

KURISHARK:

Possibly originally a portmanteau of "curious" and "shark," kurisharks are the most curious species in the seventy seas. Their curiosity manifests in biting anything that strikes them as unfamiliar, from other sharks to boats to large bubbles.

Once ubiquitous, the kurishark has decreased rapidly since a gang of kurishark youngsters dared one another into biting the Really Big Killer Sea Monster.

> |Cross-reference, THE REALLY BIG KILLER SEA MONSTER: The largest known organism in the world, or possibly an interconnected colony of organisms, the Really Big Killer Sea Monster is, as its name suggests, both enormous and monstrous. It is not generally aggressive, but it holds a grudge.|

*After swallowing whole the kurisharks that bit it,
the Really Big Killer Sea Monster developed a taste
for the sleek blue sharks, and has since been regularly
decimating the population.*

No kurisharks attacked the Clockmaker, but nor did he find a
way to escape—not in that direction nor in any other.

Three hours had passed; one remained. The Clockmaker returned unhappily to shore. He had a single option remaining, and it
wasn't one he liked to take. Vamazz the Vamazing had gotten him
into this mess—and before that, had dumped him in the soul-
stealer's dome—and before that, had left him in an oubliette!

The one bright side to asking him for help, the Clockmaker supposed, was the opportunity to ask Vamazz what he had done with
Raskolnikov. And so, reluctantly, but less reluctantly than he would
have died, the Clockmaker began to shout for help.

Vamazz did not immediately appear. The sun began to set and
the temperature drop dangerously. Soon night would fall and with
it the temperature—all the way to absolute zero. The Clockmaker's
casing would crack and fall to pieces. Only his heart would survive,
and it would roll into the heartless sea, to spend an eternity alone.
No one would mourn his tragic passing, because pirates do not
mourn, and no one else knew what was happening to him.

"Help!" the Clockmaker cried. "Help! Hel—"

His eyes caught motion and his head turned. There, not twenty
feet away, was Vamazz the Vamazing. He was not looking at the
Clockmaker, and he was not looking for the Clockmaker: he was
stopping every few feet to collect bits of rock and debris and place
them in a wicker basket. The excellent enchanter's teeth clattered
and rattled inside his skull. Snow dusted his eyelashes, and his eyebrows transmogrified into frostbrows.

"HELP!" the Clockmaker yelled.

Vamazz looked up in mild surprise. "Clockmaker!" he said.
"What are you doing here? This climate is by no means conducive
to continued health, and you do not appear to have a boat." He
frowned, and his voice became stern and scolding. "You may be

metal, but you aren't invulnerable. Coming here was highly irresponsible and reprehensible of you, and there is absolutely no excuse for it."

The Clockmaker began to explain, but Vamazz the Vamazing held up a hand to stop him. "I'll hear it later; it's far too cold to chat now." He spread out his fingers, tipped his palm sharply, and proclaimed, "Flura! Blura! Stora! Vamazz!"

The Clockmaker arrived in a flash in Balmas, that most marvelous cloud city vacation destination, with its many colored lights, its perpetual pleasant dry warmth, its free electricity and universal wealth. He spent an idyllic few weeks resting and resetting from pirate-mode before discovering the cause of Balmas's beauty: the enslavement of Vomisan Glimmer Stars.

VOMISAN GLIMMER STARS:

Typically used to refer to the stars that once resided in a cluster of constellations in the very center of the Vomisa quadrant.

A peaceful race of pinkish glimmer stars, Vomisans have no natural defenses aside from their great beauty, which they use to beguile enemies into friends—and into protecting them, if need be.

This technique worked so gorgeously for over four billion years that surrounding constellations began to rely on the Vomisans for protection, and to turn their attention from the dangers of the galaxy to its aesthetic delights. They were therefore caught completely off-guard when the Crokilinks, who have no concept of beauty, invaded.

Desperate to protect their greatest treasure, the allies managed to hold off the Crokilinks just long enough for the Vomisan stars to flee. Since then, the Vomisa quadrant has been utterly ruled by the Crokilinks, and the beauty of art and music has been almost completely supplanted by the beauty of fear and violence.

But only almost, for there remain whispers of galactic folklore: *We may have succumbed, but beauty survives. Somewhere, the Vomisan Glimmer Stars still live, safe and oh-so beautiful.*

Since it was not tourist season, and the Clockmaker was the only newcomer, it didn't take long for the authorities to pin the resulting disappearances on him. There was only one possible punishment for such treachery: the Clockmaker was hurled off the side of the cloud . . . during the daytime, when no star could come to his rescue.

Vamazz the Vamazing listened to the Clockmaker's dry rendition of an otherwise exciting rescue mission with interest, once he'd caught the Clockmaker mid-plummet.

"I'll have to have a word with them," he said, without specifying any whos or whats or whens or whys.

"I wanted to ask," the Clockmaker interjected. "Where is—"

"In the meantime," Vamazz went on, just as if the Clockmaker hadn't spoken, "you had better continue on your quest somewhere safe. I don't know how you keep getting yourself into trouble when I send you to the most mundane places, but I really do have better things to do than continually rescue you. Ah, I know: Penneng! Vuroom! Blook! Vamazz!"

The Clockmaker arrived in a sleepy little town around noon. No one seemed interested in him, being too busy sleepwalking everywhere. But as soon as evening fell, the townsfolk awoke with ravenous eyes and exactly one target in mind. The Clockmaker fled, but the vampiric lopers were as swift as he. "I am clockwork!" he yelled at them. "I am not a fleshy being, and I have no blood!"

"Then we will tear you apart!" they snarled. "We will take your metal and use it to build ovens to roast fleshy beings!"

The Clockmaker redoubled his speed, but other vampires had somehow gotten ahead of him. He had no choice; he had to call for help or be destroyed. "Vamazz!" he shouted. "Help! Help!"

He nearly tripped over the awesome augurer, who was gathering tiny white flowers into a bouquet in the woods. When Vamazz saw the Clockmaker, he smiled. "What's this?"

"Vampires!"

"Really?" Vamazz asked. "Fascinating; I have been wanting to speak with some vampires. But I hardly think this is a place for you." He tilted his hand and said some words . . .

And the Clockmaker arrived at a farm. The broadly smiling farmers with screaming eyes welcomed him with kind words that did not cease even when they locked him in the conversion machine that would make the Clockmaker exactly as they were. The Clockmaker barely croaked out a single "Help!" before the gag smothered him. He wished bleakly that he had thought to call for help earlier, for surely Vamazz would have no time to rescue him—

Only to hear a muffled voice speaking strange words. A moment later, he arrived in a labyrinth of fireplaces and chimneys.

The soot monsters disguised as furry shadows trapped him in a chimney and had eaten halfway up the Clockmaker's shins before Vamazz happened to be interested in studying the composition of the soot and found him. "You are in dire need of repairs," he informed the Clockmaker. "How do you keep doing this to yourself? No, tell me later. In the meantime—" He tilted his hand, spoke four words, and teleported the Clockmaker to a clock tower.

The clockmaker who lived there with his five thousand mechanical slaves seemed very helpful at first. He provided the Clockmaker with everything he needed to exact repairs, all the while studying him to determine how best to steal the heart of crystal.

The Clockmaker figured out what was going on and bribed a merchant to smuggle him out, only to make the mistake of mentioning his heart was crafted of pure diamond. Knowing he could not overpower the clockwork man on his own, and figuring he'd have someone else do it for him, the merchant entered the Clockmaker in a gladiatorial ring. In the end, faced with a two-ton rhinosauran, the Clockmaker called for help.

Fortunately, Vamazz happened to be in the crowd of spectators. Though professing himself sorry to ruin the show, he obligingly tilted his hand and sent the Clockmaker away—

Back out to sea in the middle of a hurricane of oliphawhales, one of whom swallowed him whole. The Clockmaker lived on a houseboat in the whale's stomach for nearly two weeks before the stomach acid ate through his floorboards. With no other option before him, he called for help, only to be magicked away to . . .

The mountains of Whair, where Hither and Yon found him.

Hither and Yon were the heads of the most ferocious giant ever to giant. Their booming fee-fi-fo-fums melted earwax, and their breath shriveled paint, plants, and potatoes with equal vigor. Their arguments made the earth tremble crevasses out of mountains and mountains out of crevasses, and their tears of laughter contaminated fresh water with salt for a hundred miles in every direction. There was nothing the heads would not eat, as long as it was or had once been alive. They ate fleas off each other's heads and pliosaurs directly from the ocean. They munched monkey shrimp, pirates (living and zombified), grasshoppers, and, when they could get them, other giants. Carbon-based life forms were no yummier to them than silicon-based or fluorine-based or metal-based—nor any less. In fact, it couldn't be said that Hither and Yon particularly enjoyed any of their food or even tasted it, so constantly did they pour it down their throats, never pleased, never full, never satisfied.

Trapped in one of their cages, the Clockmaker found himself once again with no way to escape, no choice but to call for help.

The giant turned his yellow eyes, large as swimming pools, on their collection of cages. Without hesitation, the giant lifted the first cage, opened its door, and upended it over Yon's mouth. Birds, deer, wolves, and raccoons tumbled down between the terrible teeth. Most of them lost consciousness immediately once they breathed in Yon's foul breath; the remainder chirped and howled and screeched until the chomping teeth silenced them.

The second cage contained hundreds of wood sprites. The giant tipped this cage over Hither's mouth and crunched down.

The third cage was the Clockmaker's. The giant plucked it up as easily as the Clockmaker might lift a twig or a feather, and opened the cage door. The animals in there with him immediately fainted at the breath, but the Clockmaker remained alert. He tensed, perhaps to try to make a run for it, but he must have known there was no way he could survive; if he fell to the floor from this distance, he'd crash into a million pieces. Vamazz the Vamazing was his only hope. So why didn't he call for help? He couldn't *want* to be munched and crunched and digested. What was he thinking?

Maybe there was something wrong with him; he had certainly endured a lot lately, and without much opportunity to rest and repair. Maybe he was hurt. Maybe his voice box had shattered.

Surely, he could not have *forgotten* to cry for help. Could fear be freezing his voice?

Clockmaker!

Time froze in one eternal second. The Clockmaker's eyes whipped back and forth, but he could see no source for the voice. As he was a Perpetuan, and therefore time-attuned, he recognized immediately that time had frozen. But how could time have frozen? What magic was so extraordinarily powerful that it could change the way the universe worked?

"Hello?" he said hesitantly, respectfully.

Vamazz the Vamazing is able to survive an encounter with Hither and Yon, though you are not. You should sum-

123

mon him.

The Clockmaker seemed so stunned by this revelation that he could not immediately speak.

Look, if you can't call him, I will—

"No!" the Clockmaker cried.

Excuse me?

"Please, do not call him!"

But . . . why not?

"Because he will only send me somewhere worse!"

Worse than *this*?

"Yes!"

Impossible. You are doomed. Hither and Yon are about to eat you. What could be worse?

"I do not know," the Clockmaker said devoutly, "and I do not want to find out."

The Clockmaker had a point: every time Vamazz had rescued him, he had ended up somewhere worse. But wasn't he being unfair to Vamazz? The wonderful wizard had never meant him any harm.

But perhaps we are the unfair ones. Perhaps the Clockmaker had a daring, dramatic plan of escape full of action and pathos and quick thinking. A plan one could hardly wait to witness.

Except . . .

Except then we might never find out what was *worse than this*, and I don't know about you, but I find that notion utterly irresistible. Curiosity always was my downfall.

"I am not dead yet," the Clockmaker pointed out, although he had no reason to think anyone was still listening. "Until I am, there is hope. Maybe I will slip through the giant's teeth and make a home in its stomach until I can escape. Or maybe I will snag at something in its mouth and so save myself. Please, do not call him."

The "him" in question was, at present, in his bedroom, brushing his magnificent mane of sapphire hair. By *complete coincidence* and *no interference from any outside force*, he suddenly wondered what the Clockmaker was up to. He'd been distracted and half-asleep when last he'd been pulled away from his desperately earned bed to rescue the Clockmaker's sorry self, and he couldn't quite recall where he'd sent him.

Vamazz stirred his pinky finger over the surface of his Magic Mirror of Spying on People and saw the scene: the cage tipping back over Yon's gaping maw, the Clockmaker valiantly clinging on, the giant shaking him free.

Oh, no! How appalling! He had to rescue him!

"Again," Vamazz murmured pointedly, but he dutifully spun into action. In fact, he hadn't moved so quickly since Maxwell had nearly burned the crescent cookies, the ones with the sparkly red sugar topping. He snapped out a train of thunderous words and puffed away with a strong aroma of turquoise and the sensation of wool scratching the tender skin of one's cheek.

Time unfroze, and the Clockmaker tumbled directly into Yon's mouth. But as those terrible teeth began to slam shut, something very peculiar occurred: Yon's jaw stuck open. Someone had braced it with a staff of light and darkness, neither of which is particularly edible. Vamazz the Vamazing, riding on a guitar signed by a very confused, not-yet-cheese-eating Ivan the Mild, caught the Clockmaker with one hand.

"This is ridiculous," he informed the Clockmaker, sounding harassed. "I have loads of important business I can't attend to, because I'm too busy running after you! I've had enough! This is final! I'm not letting you out of my sight again until you can rescue yourself instead of bothering me every ten minutes!"

10

The Vtopese Citadel

Clouds hung low over the trembling earth, grumbling as they bumped and shuffled along, sparking arguments that arced between sky and ground in lopsided pitchforks of searing flame. No other light pierced the obstreperous firmament. The moon, peeved, stumped away to sulk. The stars, offended, called up their agents to cancel the gig.

It was, in short, a dark and stormy night.

The *reason* it was a dark and stormy night was that Vamazz had declared it to be so, and everything in the citadel, in the air around the citadel and the clouds above it, down the scraggy cliff that explained how Vamazz had so proficiently scaled up to the Tomb of Ego the Maniac, and throughout the Vtop countryside below . . . everything functioned by Vamazz's rules.

When Vamazz sulked, such as when the price of confectioner's sugar unexpectedly elevated or the toffee mountain was discovered by a group of children and summarily snarfed, chilling mist coated the land, squirmed through door cracks, and invaded dry firewood. When Vamazz bounced with glee, the sun smiled away the mist and bathed the land in its pleasantly warm glow. Anger scorched the clouds away and withered basil plants potted on windowsills. Thoughtful calm led to crystalline nights lit by the moon's pale radiance, the most poetic sort of nights for dancing around fairy circles and gathering blood-red berries in midnight woods. And when Inspiration grasped his brain with stinky tendrils and he retired to his uppermost laboratory, thunder clashed and lightning flashed and coyotes howled at the veiled moon.

Vtop natives who visited other lands found the wider weather patterns unnerving in the extreme. "How do you know your sorcerer's moods, if not by the weather? But how do you stay safe, if not through the protection of a sorcerer? Do you mean you might simply get any weather at any time, without rhyme or meter or alliteration? How nightmarish!"

Nightmarish was the strongest word in any Vtopese's vocabulary. Vamazz seldom had nightmares. He dreamt often, but although it is sometimes inconvenient to find yourself singing everything, encountering giant praying mantises handing you holy pamphlets written entirely in mantis language without even a dictionary to help you translate, turning into a lapdog, or being able to fly by swimming through air, it is never actively harmful and may in fact be as metaphorically charming as it is literally.

Even when Vamazz had what you or I might call a nightmare, but which is actually no more than an unpleasant dream, things weren't so bad. No one got in trouble for forgetting about a test on days like this, or for showing up late to work or for going about without any pants on. In fact, the Vtopese laughed about it and built public toilets on every block (so that it wasn't possible not to be able to find one) and boasted about how many beetles they'd eaten this time.

Nightmares, though . . . nightmares were something else. Folk still whispered about the Nightmare of '135 and shuddered in horror at the memory of their neighbors' soulless eyes, the uncertainty of who was possessed, and the suspicion that it was everyone—including you.

It had come as no relief when the demons had dropped their guises and invaded in person, with their acid bombs and flaming axes. You could trust no one not to betray you, and you found yourself betraying those you loved without ever wanting to, screaming inside your mind to *stop, stop, stop!* but being unable to obey.

In the way of nightmares, time had stretched, contorted, and mocked a single night into months and months. Only when Vamazz had woken the next morning did the nightmare end, and even then its echoes resounded deafeningly.

The Vtopese did not blame Vamazz for the nightmare, or they didn't after the trauma had faded slightly and Vamazz had done all in his power as a wonderful wizard, majestic magus, superior sorcerer, excellent enchanter, awesome augurer, mediocre magician, dauntless diviner, nervy necromancer, and thupreme thaumaturge to heal them. The Vtopese understood that Vamazz had suffered through the nightmare even as they had, and those who did not move away contented themselves by sending representatives to demand safeguards.

"We could not leave or call for help or wake you," they said. "We need an automatic system, one that cannot be trapped by a nightmare."

"I'll set something up," Vamazz promised.

"We want an automatic alert," the representatives pressed, "sent to Galapagos."

"How dare—"

The representatives crossed their arms, and Vamazz pacified his bristling eyelashes. "Fine," he snapped. "I'll do it. But in return, you will *not* mention that personage again."

The citadel's interior, far from being the calm in the tornado and therefore less vulnerable to Vamazz's moods, dreams, and sense of dramatic timing, felt them ten times worse. Nowhere was safe, not in the potato cupboard, not in the syrup shower, and not in the flower press. Flashes of damp, heat, and brutal cold withered those potatoes or primed them to sprout; the shower froze and boiled its water with malicious glee; and the flowers waved decorated fronds while threatening to wilt.

Vamazz's home was definitely not what the Clockmaker would have expected, if he had had time and leisure to expect anything before being whisked off there. For one thing, it was a citadel rather than a villa or vernacular or valace. For another, it primarily comprised peach stone, damp, and fungus. For a third, there were no books anywhere, magical or otherwise.

Possibly, there once had been books, but the damp had turned them into mushroom food long ago—and there were mushrooms *everywhere.* Mushrooms lined the rooms and corridors. Mushrooms spiraled up the spiral stairs and painted window sills black and white and twined tendrils up onto the glass to form formly formations. Mushrooms squashed and flew beneath the Clockmaker's metal feet, and the balconies were shaded not by stone but by the brown-gray gills of massive mushrooms.

Vamazz and the Clockmaker were both too heavy to be bothered by the mushy mushroom carpet, but Maxwell—whom Vamazz introduced as his factotum, and who indeed seemed to do everything Vamazz asked him—slipped and slid and skated down stairs and through rooms with his arms spread perpendicular and his weight leaned forward.

The Clockmaker wasn't entirely sure what to make of Maxwell, who in addition to being inclined to tease him, was a slikerty.

SLIKERTY:

The spirit of a drowned child. Rare and mirage-like in appearance, slikerties roam the land in damp misery, leaving muddy footsteps wherever they go. As most parents have lost the ability to see slikerties, being too afraid the same will happen to their own offspring, a high percentage of slikerty activity (e.g., stained carpets and mud trails) is blamed on innocent children.

Although occasionally inconvenient, slikerties are ultimately harmless. Those compassionate souls wishing to help them may do so as follows:

1) Banishment. Slikerties may be banished by sprinkling them with lilac-infused magnesium sulfate during a total lunar eclipse. Other-

wise, they will naturally dissipate under the next total solar eclipse.

2) Embodiment. Slikerties may be embodied during any harvest moon, while both moon and sun are visible in the sky, by being completely doused in petroleum jelly.

Banished slikerties are never seen again. Embodied slikerties generally become attached to their embodier, adopting him as a parent or master until the next solar eclipse or until the embodier passes away. At that point, some slikerties adopt the embodier's family. Those who do not generally return to their disembodied form and roam the land in damp misery once more.

While Vamazz slept, Maxwell often followed the Clockmaker around, watching him with suspicious eyes. This was wholly unnecessary, because, true to his word, Vamazz never let the Clockmaker out of his sight. During his waking hours, Vamazz demanded the Clockmaker go wherever he go and do whatever he asked. When Vamazz wanted a bit of sleep or privacy, he plucked out one of his eyeballs and set it to float over the Clockmaker's left shoulder.

"Keeping an eye on you, is he?" cackled Maxwell, the first time he saw this.

"Above me," the Clockmaker corrected severely.

The Clockmaker spent a lot of his time wandering the citadel, in his early days with Vamazz. From Maxwell, who was willing to show off, he learned that Vamazz hadn't built the citadel himself; it had already been old, damp, and haunted when he'd moved in. Aside from a spot or two of mold in the closets and trailing up the walls and down the toilets, fungus had not played an integral role in its architecture.

"Then Vamazz must have wanted the mushrooms," the Clockmaker concluded. "Why?"

Maxwell shrugged. "That," he said, "is inexplicable to anyone without a turquoise mind. But he does like them, and so you'd better not try to get rid of them!"

The Clockmaker's father had always taught him to keep the shop spotless, and none of his adventures had ever successfully undermined that preference. But, remembering with a pang how precious Sharpig's eggplants had been to him, the Clockmaker reluctantly concurred.

The citadel's shape was that of a Gordian knot, its corridors really a single corridor that wound, jerked, doubled back, dodged down, and reared up at random. Rooms clung on to it with doors, trap doors, chutes, secret passageways, arches, removable stones, puzzle boxes, riddling knockers, and a dozen other contrivances meant to baffle, enlighten, tease, and challenge the inhabitants.

Neither Vamazz nor Maxwell had any difficulty maneuvering from the kitchens to the brimstone laboratory to the observation hub to the experimental mushroom tent, because Vamazz and Maxwell simply went wherever they intended without considering the bits that came in between. The Clockmaker, who marked and memorized every step, took five times longer to arrive anywhere, assuming he arrived at all, which he frequently did not.

"You need to let go," Vamazz advised. "Don't think about it. Forget the path; concentrate on anything else. It doesn't like being noticed."

"I think about everything I do and notice everywhere I go," said the Clockmaker, "unless I am greatly distressed—and I prefer not to be."

"He doesn't know anything," Maxwell said scornfully. "He can't maneuver a hallway, and you expect him to be able to learn magic? He could no more weave a wonder than prance a dance!"

"I could teach him to dance, if I wanted to," said Vamazz. "As for magic—we'll begin tomorrow."

"In the meantime," said the Clockmaker, "I would like to know where Raskolnikov is."

He had attempted to ask this question several times since arriving at the citadel, but Vamazz had always been distracted or inexplicably deaf. Now, he looked questioningly at the Clockmaker.

"The pycckni dwarf hamster," the Clockmaker reminded him. "He was with me in the cheese."

"I know who Raskolnikov is," Vamazz said mildly.

"Then where is he?"

Vamazz rolled his tongue beneath his bottom lip, contemplating the Clockmaker. "Unharmed," he said. "Protected by a person I will not discuss. Beyond that ... consider this an incentive to learn magic. If you learn enough, you'll be able to find him for yourself."

And with that, the Clockmaker had to be content.

Vamazz's lessons began, ordinarily enough, in front of a blackboard. For the occasion, he had stripped off the bulkier parts of his armor and chains, leaving behind the burnt-orange-and-blue robe and frilly white shirt. He did not need the robe for warmth; he simply enjoyed the way it swirled impressively around his feet as he strode across the room, gesticulating broadly.

During his classes, he took his topics in the order in which they occurred to him. "Augury!" he might announce. "A fatuous discipline revered by kings who believe that the flight patterns of seagulls can predict whether they will win a war. A classic mistake— confusing correlation with causation. Bird patterns do not predict outcomes; they determine them. Any simpleton can read patterns, but it takes an awesome augurer like me to predict or influence them."

Although he never pretended humility, in this case Vamazz was, by calling himself an awesome augurer, simply giving the correct title for his level of proficiency. He had passed through the apprentice, adept, and amazing stages to the very highest augurer rank: awesome. In fact, Vamazz held the highest rank in every magical discipline save two: nervy necromancer was one step below the lauded neurotic, and mediocre magician barely one step above mundane.

"My instructor in magicianship," Vamazz explained stiffly, when the Clockmaker dared ask, "was only a mundane magician; I have surpassed her. I could improve further, but why bother? Magicianship is only an inferior form of magusry."

The Clockmaker took the hint. But his silence did not stop him from wondering whether Vamazz really had no desire to be able to pull a comet out of his triangular blue hat as well as rabbits and doves.

In addition to his many lectures on augury, necromancy, and magicianship, Vamazz covered the other magical disciplines. At present, and until he looked into magic, the Clockmaker could only perform the magic that he learned while inside the citadel. Technically, during his apprenticeship, he was accessing Vamazz's magic with Vamazz's permission and not his own magic at all—but Vamazz assured the Clockmaker that the skills he learned would transfer once he went inside magic.

"I understood that magic was looked into," the Clockmaker said, "not gone inside."

"Maybe looking into magic is enough for paltry weak warlocks and empty enchanters who wish for nothing greater than to practice their trade in a circus stall," Vamazz replied, "but you are going to be and do much more, my boy."

Another time, he began to tell the Clockmaker about elemental magic.

"Or what some care to call the elements," Vamazz sniffed, and broke off into a dissertation on the composition of reality and the various pleats of reality's petticoat.

"I know about the Phantom Plane," the Clockmaker hazarded—"what Master Nindi called the plane of soul magic."

"Yes, I've heard about his theories," Vamazz said.

The Clockmaker's heart soared. Who but Raskolnikov could have told him?

"But they are limited. The Phantom Plane is a simple semi-post-life-sideways reflection. What of the other planes—Pre-life, Life, Perception (including Deception, Delusion, and Discussion), and Empathy? What of all the hundreds of others?" Vamazz shook his head sadly. "So many believe that the elements that make up the universe are water, earth, air, and fire. Many others break these down into their components: hydrogen, oxygen, carbon, and so on. And then, with the compulsiveness of true compulsives, they break them further down into electrons and protons and *space*—mostly space, truth be told. And what do they think space is made of?"

"Nothing," the Clockmaker guessed.

"Nothing," Vamazz agreed. "According to these oh-so-clever morons, the universe is composed somewhat of buzzing buttons but mostly of nothing. They're as bad as the philosophers!"

There was a long digression there, about what it was that philosophers were so bad at, but eventually they came back to the main topic, and the Clockmaker asked, "What is the universe made up of?"

"What are hopes made up of?" Vamazz said. "What is love made up of? What is nonsense made up of? Those questions are meaningless, because they don't pertain to the subject at hand. All these scientists and philosophers are so busy asking *what* the universe is made up of that they don't bother to ask *whether* asking what the universe is made up of is a coherent question!"

On yet other occasions, and in no order that the Clockmaker could determine, Vamazz shared the history of magic. Some of this he did by throwing mushrooms at the Clockmaker. Without either the mushrooms growing any bigger or the Clockmaker growing any smaller, the fungus enveloped him. It cut off his senses entirely—every sense except his sense of imagination. On this, Vamazz played his violin, striking up brutal imagery and sunshine, providing orchestration to the scenes depicted. Some of the history, he shared through epic songs, traditional dances, and whispered epic poetry. Some, he simply told the Clockmaker.

Not every lesson was held in a classroom, of course; Vamazz was an extremely busy man. He discussed new spells as he invented them or showed the Clockmaker how to whisk ancient, cobwebby charms into new life. He lectured through lunch and taught at tea. And, most importantly, he took the Clockmaker with him wherever and for whatever reason he went.

The Clockmaker learned the ins and outs, ups and downs, rights and lefts of each discipline whether right side up or upside down or spinning—and since he had a diamond tourbillon heart, he never grew dizzy or lost time over them, although much of the information, he learned without understanding. He would finally understand it a year later—only to realize, a year after that, that he had not really understood it at all, and wasn't positive he could ever understand it or, indeed, that it was the sort of thing for which understanding was a relevant factor.

Vamazz smiled when the Clockmaker expressed these thoughts. This smile baffled the Clockmaker for another year, until he realized that the topics he had agonized over and thought indecipherably complicated were in fact the simplest of magics, whereas the ones he'd thought simple—such as lighting a candle with the snap of his fingers—were so vastly deep and boilingly wide that drinking them for a year could consume barely a drop of the ocean, and anything he removed would flow seamlessly back into place.

"But if it is that complicated," the Clockmaker said to Vamazz, "why did I learn it first? Why did you not start with the simple things?"

Vamazz blinked up from the pocket watch he'd been poking at, under the Clockmaker's guidance. "How can anyone understand what is simple before they understand what is complex? Being given flowers is pleasing; that is simple. But how can one understand that pleasure without understanding about beauty, interpersonal attachments, affection, cultural tradition surrounding flowers, the concept of a gift, and—" He paused, eyebrows coming together in thought. "Have you ever been given flowers?"

"No," the Clockmaker admitted.

"I see." Vamazz turned the topic after that, but at dinner he presented the Clockmaker with a handpicked bouquet of forget-me-nots.

The Clockmaker was more touched than he could express. Without having intended to, he found himself spending the evening walking the village at the base of the cliff, learning the lore of forget-me-nots, how to care for them, and how to dry them into preservation when they began to wilt.

After the Clockmaker's first year in the citadel, Vamazz had extended his magic blanket to the edge of the village, allowing the Clockmaker to teleport down and back instead of scaling the cliff. The villagers had grown used to his presence, for Vamazz sent him for anything too distant or substantial for Maxwell to carry and to settle disputes (or to bring the details back to Vamazz, if he could not settle them) and to solve village problems that could be fixed by main strength, mechanical manipulation, or musical prowess: lyric wax music to cure insomnia, music box music to feed the hungry of spirit, and pirate shanties to fill the dance hall.

By this point, Vamazz had grown lax enough to only have half an eye over the Clockmaker's shoulder, or to have an eye on him only half the time. Not infrequently, the Clockmaker realized he wasn't being watched at all, and strange possibilities welled up inside him.

"You could escape," Maxwell suggested one such evening, sliding slyly up to him. "If you went now, without telling him, he wouldn't follow you. He wouldn't know where you were, unless you called his name. You've been hanging around for months and months, neglecting your friends, not even trying to look for them. They might be in danger!"

"I could look for my friends," the Clockmaker agreed, "but I would not be able to find them. I do not now believe that the Land of the Purple Ring can be found by ordinary means, and I have no information with which to begin looking for Raskolnikov—but in any case, Vamazz assures me he is safe."

Besides, he added to himself—silently, because he was aware that Maxwell's paternal jealousy wore pitchers for ears—*leaving without saying goodbye would hurt his feelings*.

"I will not go," he said aloud. "Vamazz yet has much to teach me—and I wish to learn."

Here is some more of what the Clockmaker learned:

WIZARDRY:

In wizardry, everything must be performed as quickly as possible—at a whizz. A slow-spoken spell or lazy gesture will not only not work, it will actively offend the magic. Hence why lighting a candle, which might involve hand twirls in elemental magic or a canted "Dearest candle / set alight / your waiting wick / to banish night" in enchantment, involves only snapped fingers in wizardry.

Although the speediest of the disciplines, wizardry is littered with wheeled plastic toys for the careless amateur. Snapping the fingers one way will result in the desired effect, but in another way will instead ignite the fireplace, the kitchen table, or the snapper. Wizardry has caused the unintentional maiming, mangling, and death of more practitioners than any other discipline save sorcery.

SORCERY:

The imbuing and the utilization of imbued objects. Sorcerers regularly scour crypts, temples, palaces, and their neighbors' dustbins for magical objects they can subject to their will. Since most magical objects have a will of their own—and are usually only available to the sorcerer because they have destroyed, devoured, or driven mad their previous masters—this sort of scavenging is inherently and intensely dangerous. Any weak-willed sorcerer will soon find himself being controlled by his imbued objects rather than the other way around.

More advanced sorcerers are able to imbue their

own objects by capturing and distilling magical plants, creatures, and spirits. The humble sorcerer knows his limits; the proud sorcerer seeks out creatures beyond his ability to control, and inevitably becomes subject to them—unless he also happens to be a therionologist.

THERIONOLOGY:

Specialization in communication with and control over animals, utilizing both mental and physical speech, expressions, and gestures. Therionologists may build an empathetic connection with even the most hostile creature, with only these exceptions:

- Fully sentient beings.
- Brainless beings. Therionologists generally can form no meaningful connection with, for example, viruses, and thus make poor magical healers (although excellent veterinary diagnosticians).
- Trolmoers.
- Non-living animals. This category is, unsurprisingly, reserved for necromancers.

NECROMANCY—

Actually, the Clockmaker met a necromancer very early in his tutelage, which brings us full circle to:

It was a dark and stormy night.

The Clockmaker, mincing experimental mushrooms into 1/13-inch cubes at Vamazz's behest, used the rumbling and crashing as percussive backing to his continuing imagination expansion project. With ever-varying tone and tune, he belted one of the rhymes his father had taught him:

Little Tommy Tompkins went to the grave,
Singing to himself, "Now aren't I brave?
I'm not afraid of the walking dead;
I won't be scared by revizited."

Little Tommy Tompkins got a surprise,
When revizited came to suck out his eyes.
Only black holes remained in his head—
He should have stayed away from revizited.

Now Tommy Tompkins is in that grave—
Funny how stupid is the same as brave.
If only he'd been good and gone to bed,
He wouldn't have been gotten by revizited.

It took only two repetitions of the song to drive away Maxwell. As the Clockmaker began on his thirty-second repetition, his percussion section crashed into a constant deafening roar that shook the earth for a full three minutes before abruptly splintering into tens of thousands of shards of ice.

Hail slapped, smacked, struck, and sizzled through the citadel roof, through the uppermost floor below, and down two levels until it bounced on the mushroom tent and rolled to the floor, where it released a strong stench of roasted mushroom.

Dropping his knife, the Clockmaker dove under the cutting table, confused and alarmed and having no idea what to do—for this was far before he learned any shielding or protection charms. Was Vamazz trying to kill him? This was worse than the dream Vamazz had had last night—and that had involved waltzing stools!

"VAMAZZ!" Maxwell bellowed, voice bouncing into walls as he skated through trap doors, around riddle arches, and up the laundry chute. "VAMAZZ, STOP IT! YOU'RE KILLING THE MUSH-ROOMS!"

The hail abruptly shut off. Every midair hunk of ice evaporated on the spot, and the landed hail melted away to moisturize the poor mangled mushrooms.

Light flared, and suddenly Vamazz landed in the mushroom tent. Flame swooshed beneath his feet and flared from his fingertips. Turquoise light shone from his eyes, and chains flailed out from his form like hissing snakes, their flaming ends dotted with two black specks like eyes. Power sloshed off him in waves, raising wind and causing the experimental mushrooms to shrivel in fear and awe.

"Get out from under that table," Vamazz ordered, and his voice too was distant—a vast thing from a great distance, as if, were it any closer, it would crumble the world as Time crumbled buildings in her wake. "You're coming with me."

The Clockmaker had never seen Vamazz so plainly furious. In his fury, Vamazz did not even use his ordinary routine of tipping his hand and uttering magical words; instead, he simply rushed flaming turquoise around them like a cloak and *yanked* what felt like a very, very long distance. They landed with a sort of whoosh in a copse of slender trees with crackly bark the deep reddish-brown of a scab and about the same texture. Instead of pine needles or leaves, long spines dangled from their thin, grasping branches. Midnight-brown sap oozed from each spine tip.

"He's been here, too," Vamazz said. His voice had gone flat, and the Clockmaker knew that something about the trees had made him angrier than ever.

The Clockmaker had never seen trees anything like these. He drew a spine close, flipping on his highest magnification.

"Don't!" Vamazz shouted belatedly, as some of the sap dripped onto the Clockmaker's palm. The Clockmaker obediently released the spine, but instead of springing back, it plunged forward, scoring a brown streak along his wrist.

The Clockmaker stared at the scratch, aghast. He flipped his gut compartment open to reach for the repair kit.

"Don't," Vamazz ordered, and the Clockmaker saw that the color had seeped from his face. "Let me."

"With respect," the Clockmaker replied, "I prefer to perform my own repairs."

"Don't be a fool," Vamazz snarled back. "I will *not* have you spreading that around, infecting everyone around you. You're lucky not to be dead!"

Realizing that more was going on than he knew, the Clockmaker extended his wrist toward the thupreme thaumaturge, to do as he would.

Shuddering rather, and careful not to touch the sap, Vamazz passed his hands over and around the affected appendage, singing wordless notes outside of music.

The sap hissed, turned toxic yellow, and evaporated. Then the whole of the Clockmaker's arm turned white hot. He cried out, lest he melt, but the arm was already cooling. In a few seconds, just slowly enough that his delicate innards did not crack, it was barely more than warm.

"From now on," said Vamazz, "touch *nothing* without my say-so. Understood?"

The Clockmaker nodded.

"Good. Follow me." Vamazz marched eastward through the copse, shooting fiery glares at any spines rash enough to dart at him.

The Clockmaker followed in his footsteps, thinking. He kept seeing faces in the nests of spines and limbs, but whenever he turned to look, there was only plant life. Was this an effect of practicing his imagination—or something to do with whatever had made Vamazz so furious?

"I *warned* him," Vamazz burst out suddenly. "I told him that if he didn't stop, I'd be back. He promised he would stop—pretended to be cowed. But you see this? You *see* this? Ten times worse than before. A hundred times worse! He's gathering power. Thinks if he gets enough, he can defeat me."

"Can he?"

Vamazz sent the Clockmaker a scornful look. *"No."* His mouth turned down, forehead creased. "At least, I don't think so. Last time I met him, definitely not. But this . . . I meant to transport us well outside of his circle of influence, even allowing for expansion."

He marched on. As they went, the trees grew broader and taller, and the atmosphere grew denser, malice seeping toward them like the foundation of despair. But Vamazz was doing something, too. His eyes gleamed with magic, and the Clockmaker could feel him tugging, drawing in power not from the trees, but over and around and beneath them somehow, in the spaces malice had missed.

The Clockmaker hurried to keep close on Vamazz's heels, which seemed to help hold the pressure at bay.

They emerged from the copse at the edge of a river that time had dug down fifteen feet. Something about the sight of that river, running upstream with pained gasps, sent storm clouds across Vamazz's cheeks. "Gaspard!" he bellowed over the sound of the water, gravel roughening his voice. "I warned you!"

The river spanned perhaps a hundred paces, its current swift but not ferocious, splashing against boulders and swirling in curlicues of confused current in the nooks and crannies of the tree at its center.

It was something else, that tree. Its root system must have stretched the width of the river in both directions, the smaller trees its disreputable offspring. Continually moisturized and fed, it glistened red—and redder still in the ruddy glow of sunset.

The atmosphere of malice originated at that tree; evil pulsed out like a heartbeat, sickening everything it touched. Fish swimming too near it were caught by it and slurped away. The water around the roots polluted and sickened everything it touched. Against the vibrant sky, the tree's branches dangled bundles that swayed in a light breeze.

Vamazz hissed between his teeth.

"Are we meant to go to the tree?" the Clockmaker asked doubtfully. "I could wade, if you like, and carry you on my shoulders. I am waterproof to thirty fathoms."

Vamazz shot him a quick, calculating glance. "He wouldn't expect that," he allowed, "and it would be better not to attempt to reach him by magical means; that would make it too easy for him to set a trap. And yet I would prefer to make him come to us, away from the source of his power."

He raised his voice again. "What is this cowardice, Gaspard? Will you face me—or do you know you're still too weak?"

No reply came that the Clockmaker could hear, except that the wind picked up, waving spines and shaking bundles as if in laughter.

"I should burn it down from here," Vamazz grumbled. "But if there's any chance that even one of them remains uncontaminated . . ." His lips compressed. "When we arrive, leave the necromancer to me. Remove as many hanging beings as you can, but do *not* touch the spines."

With that, Vamazz sprang lightly onto the Clockmaker's shoulders, and stood balanced on the sleek metal without apparent effort.

Heart spinning, the Clockmaker shut his ears and waded forward.

The current ran stronger than he had expected—much stronger—and he could feel Vamazz's strength supporting him as he dug his feet between stones and pushed forward. Vamazz was keeping out most of the pressing malice, too. The Clockmaker was grateful, but couldn't help wondering what would happen if Vamazz were distracted.

The water rose over the Clockmaker's chest and soaked Vamazz's ankles, but not long after it completely enveloped the Clockmaker, his feet found massive roots and he walked along them. Higher and higher he went once more. A chilly breeze whisked the top of his head.

Vamazz shifted then, and the Clockmaker thought by the vibrations that he must have said something, though he could not hear what—and then Vamazz's weight swung off him. The Clockmaker clambered unhampered out of the water and onto the mesh of roots and aggregate and magic that surrounded the tree.

Vamazz stood nearby, head tilted back. The Clockmaker tilted his head back too, and saw their foe for the first time.

The necromancer Gaspard had until lately been a man of moderate weight; but now stretch marks ran in lines across his fat face and hands. The rest of his bloated body was hidden behind a thick wool gown; but despite this, tremors of cold shot through him at irregular intervals. Angry veins throbbed in his neck and forehead, and he swayed slightly on the tree limbs that supported him.

"All the rutabagas in the world won't save you, Gaspard,"

Vamazz was saying. "You've only gone and poisoned yourself." His gleaming eyes caught the Clockmaker, and he mouthed, *Get them down!*

The Clockmaker nodded subtly and began looking.

This close, he saw that the bundles he'd spotted from shore were in fact creatures impaled on spines. They were dead, every one of them; and with a start, the Clockmaker realized that he recognized some of the faces from the trees.

The Clockmaker could not climb, but he could stretch up his arm and tug down the lower branches close enough to slide the creatures off the spines. Down here were only the dumb animals—the deer and squirrels and foxes and trout that were all that Gaspard had been able to capture when last Vamazz had been here, when the tree had been much smaller and the necromancer's power much weaker—for evil trees such as these grow from the top up.

The Clockmaker pulled a coyneep from the spine with the loud slurping of released suction.

Gaspard cried out in anger and fear and turned his way, fat hands forming claws; but Vamazz shouted a string of Words, forcing Gaspard to focus on him instead.

From this, the Clockmaker understood two things: that Gaspard did not want the spines defrocked, and that it was desperately urgent that the Clockmaker defrock them as quickly as possible.

He moved into top speed, emptying the spines along that branch and then along the next and dropping each dead creature into the screeching, boiling water. He cleared off every branch he could reach and then stopped to wait for further instructions.

Glistening sweat wet Gaspard's face, and the turquoise light blurred even stronger in Vamazz's. The Clockmaker could feel their magics battle, but he could not understand the fine details, could not parse the leaning pressure or the sudden giving away, could not do anything useful but wait and watch as sweat waterfalled from Gaspard in greater and greater quantities until he imploded, sloshing away into the tree's ravenous bark.

"Thank you," Vamazz told the Clockmaker. Then he swung into the tree and out along the branches, to examine and free every creature he found there.

He returned twenty minutes later, grim-faced and holding an infant in his arms. "The rest were contaminated beyond restoration, but we can give one family the comfort of a burial," he told the Clockmaker. He took the Clockmaker's arm, paused, and added darkly, "Once we get back to shore, I'm burning everything."

The Clockmaker met many other magicists during his years with Vamazz: good and bad and evil and just plain weird, competent and incompetent, nice and rude and ignorant and childish and entirely ridiculous.

After their encounter with Gaspard the necromancer, the Clockmaker supposed that no more wicked or powerful magicist could exist, and that there could be no magical discipline more hideously evil than necromancy. He was wrong on both points, for necromancy is no more or less inherently evil than any other sort of magic . . . and there existed such evil as lay beyond anything Gaspard could have imagined, fantasized, dreamed of, hoped for, or planned.

The curious thing was, the level of evil and the amount of power a magicist wielded were only partially correlated. True, high levels of power tended to corrupt, and few could achieve really big evils without really big magic, but they met a few small-time warlocks and augurers who were quite as evil as the evilest sorcerer Vamazz ever put down. These were the ones who could not be stopped by mere threats, who would continue doing evil even if Vamazz stripped away their magic and gave it to those who had been victimized with it—but in the latter cases, Vamazz allowed the victims to deal out their own justice, for he always believed in allowing people to deal with what they could, rather than be mollycoddled by his extremely busy self.

The Clockmaker likewise learned that, even as Gaspard's evil had not been extraordinary, nor had his power been. It had been far greater than Vamazz had expected, true, and Vamazz would have prepared rather differently had he known, but they had never been in any substantial danger. With proper preparation, Vamazz was capable of dealing with necromancers ten times Gaspard's strength. Only on two occasions, in the time the Clockmaker knew him, did Vamazz ever contact other magicists for assistance beyond what the Clockmaker and Maxwell could supply; and only once did he call for help *in medias res*.

By contrast, Vamazz was asked for help rather frequently, and he often gave it. Sometimes, this help took the form of telling the person strongly that he did not need help or that he was entirely to blame and should go apologize; but not infrequently, Vamazz went in person to sort out whatever mayhem, magicist, or monster had created the situation.

Beyond assisting them, the only times the Clockmaker met other good magicists were at parties. Vamazz constantly received invitations from the grateful, the gregarious, and the sycophantic, and he felt obliged to attend the get-togethers of his more esteemed colleagues. He himself held a bash only once a year, on the thirty-first of October. In the week preceding that date, he, Maxwell, and the Clockmaker spent every moment of free time magically expanding a room of the citadel to serve as a ballroom; and in cleaning, decorating, and otherwise impressifying the interior.

One year, an evil enchanter got word of the bash, and decided to gate-crash it and announce his world-domination scheme, only to find himself faced with the forty-three most powerful magicists in the world, every one of them furious at his impropriety. He was hit by forty-three spells at once, and all that remained of him after that was a skein of rather cheap ribbon in unsightly lime-bog green.

Of these forty-three magicists, Vamazz himself was debatably the strongest overall. But though an intensely powerful sorcerer, augurer, necromancer (he attained "neurotic" about eight months, four days, thirteen hours, and four-point-three seconds after their encounter with Gaspard), wizard, neuromancer, and all the rest, he was not always the *most* powerful in any single field. His greatest advantage, the advantage that made him so vamazing, and the advantage he passed on to the Clockmaker, was his capacity for diversity.

The Clockmaker had assumed that people who learned no magic or only one sort of magic did so for lack of teachers, lack of effort, or lack of intelligence. Then, nearly two years into his apprenticeship, Vamazz began him on therionology, and the Clockmaker found himself at a loss. He could not seem to connect to the magic, and the more he reached for it, the more slippery it became and the more difficult to see. Again and again and again and again and again the Clockmaker tried, and would probably have continued trying indefinitely had not Vamazz stopped him.

"I do not understand!" the Clockmaker cried, in deep distress. "I must be malfunctioning!"

"Nonsense," Vamazz said; "you simply aren't attuned to therionology. Don't let it worry you—you've already demonstrated an aptitude for eight types of magic, and that's seven more than most

magicists manage. We will move on to photomancy and forget therionology. I believe you are interested in your Master Nindi's magic?"

It was a good attempt at distraction, but not quite enough. The Clockmaker asked, "Is there *anyone* who can use every sort of magic?"

"Certainly," said Vamazz: "I can. And there is one other … but we don't talk about *that* one."

Over his course of study, the Clockmaker gained the following proficiencies:

1. Alchemy (3rd rank)
2. Arithmancy (4th rank)
3. Chronomancy (2nd rank)
4. Divination, specialization: astrology (4th rank)
5. Elementalism, specializations: geokinesis and electrical manipulation (3rd rank)
6. Enchantment (4th rank)
7. Light and shadow magery (4th rank)
8. Magicianship (4th rank)
9. Magusry (4th rank)
10. Mechanomancy and technomancy (2nd rank)
11. Sorcery (3rd rank)
12. Spatial manipulation (4th rank)
13. Wizardry (3rd rank)

In any field where Vamazz noticed that the Clockmaker had little potential, he merely implanted the base knowledge and then focused on more fertile ground. "You have the capacity," he told the Clockmaker, "to achieve the first rank in any of those thirteen specialties, given time. But it is clear to me that your talents do not lie in the magics to do with living beings—with animancy, therionology, blood magic, herbalism, or any of the others. Focus on what you are best at and perfect those things; the others may come with time, or they may not."

The Clockmaker knew by this that change was coming.

Vamazz had measured his progress before, but never so ruthlessly given him advice to be used in his absence.

"I have so much to learn," the Clockmaker said, a little desperately. "I have not yet achieved a first rank in anything. You could teach me yet for years and years! And in any case, you require my help. What if the Simpering Sorcerer should return in my absence? You know his voice does not affect me as it does you."

"My dear boy," said Vamazz, "if I call you, however far away you are, will you not come?"

"But I do not wish to leave."

"Wishes or no wishes, you may not and must not stay: you have unfulfilled business. First, your magic grows too weighty for me to support: you must travel into magic and unlock your own. Second, you must find your friends, as you have vowed to do."

"But I do not know how to get into magic," the Clockmaker said mulishly.

"Nonsense," Vamazz snapped. "Would you so insult my teaching as to pretend you have learned nothing? You are ready; you lack but a name. I will not have you ending your spells with 'Vamazz' forever. Imagine the confusion!"

The Clockmaker went even heavier and more unhelpful. "I have a name," he said. "I am named after my father. I am the Clockmaker."

"Are you really?" Vamazz's words cut the air, but he softened them with a sad smile. "My dear boy, when was the last time you made a clock?"

The Clockmaker stared, silent and hurt.

"If you keep a lie for your name, you will unlock your abilities under false pretenses—and you have seen where that leads."

The Clockmaker had, too many times to count. But his father—

"Do you honestly believe," asked Vamazz, "that your father would reject you even if you called yourself Fitzsnotwardpile?" He let out a sigh. "You do not have to choose your new name yet, although I would have liked to hear it. But if you do not choose it now, you must travel into magic with no name, and accept whatever name you receive there. I would ask," he added, after a moment's reflection, "that once you have your new name, you inform me of it."

The clockwork man nodded, heart too full to speak, and turned his gaze and feet to magic.

11

Magic

When he had been seventeen, the Warty Warlock—then merely a warty teenager—had caught a passing glimpse of something in a darkened window.

His first careless, arresting thought was that an animal or person had come up to the glass to peer in at him, but he soon rejected this as nonsense. It must be only his reflection, caught by the wavy distortion of uneven glass.

And yet it did not look like his reflection. It did not move as he moved closer, peering in puzzlement. It did not raise its arm, and the colors were entirely wrong. As it drew him forward over clumsy feet, he thought in astonishment, *Why, this isn't my reflection at all! It's—it's—*

In that moment, he lost whatever it was. Maybe his distraction was to blame, or maybe he had tripped over his too-large feet. Whatever had dislodged the connection, the darkened glass was merely glass, the window looking out onto nothing more extraordinary than a moonlit garden.

But from that day forward, a trickle of magic danced around the Warty Warlock's legs, as eager as a playful dog—and as loyal.

There is no single definitive method for stepping into magic. Everyone must find his own way, however tortuous, torturous, and tortoise-slow the path. The clockwork man had been telling the truth when he'd said that he did not know how to step into magic; Vamazz had never told him how, and it was not something one could know without having done it. As a 4th rank spatial manipulator, however, he had a few insightful ideas (but, alas, no Ideas) on the matter.

First, since most individuals who looked or walked into magic did so without using magic, it stood to reason that no sorcery or wizardry or necromancy or other discipline was necessary for the process, and might even be counterproductive. The clockwork man therefore transported himself to the edge of Vamazz's influence and walked until he found himself completely denuded of magical access.

Second, looking and walking into magic was something often done by accident. As in the Warty Warlock's case, this could be through a mirage, wavy glass, or some other manner of perceptional delusion. However, it must be possible to enter magic without using delusion as a crutch, for Vamazz believed the clockwork man capable of it—which meant that a man with a clockwork brain that thought only actuality and clockwork eyes that saw only reality could enter magic. As elements of perceptional delusion were the only props the clockwork man had heard of people using, and since the clockwork man could not use them, it stood to reason that no props were necessary. It was no great jump, the clockwork man concluded, to suppose that one could walk into magic from any direction, at any time, and in any way.

(He was not in fact wholly correct on this point; but as the clockwork man happened to be in a place and time and state in which transition to magic was possible, he did not discover these details until much later, and at the most inconvenient occasion imaginable—but that adventure is beyond the scope of this book, and ought not be dwelt upon at greater length at present.)

Third, if magic were a place one could look or step into at any point, it stood to reason that the only thing the clockwork man needed to do was lift up his foot and put it down, and he would be there. Putting it down left or right or forward or backward or at an angle made no sense, because he had done those things many times, and had never before stepped into magic. It must be more like using spatial magic to transport yourself from *here* to *there:* you put your foot down somewhere else, somewhere that didn't exist otherwise—perhaps the only other somewhere you could place your foot without using magic.

The clockwork man spent three hours lifting and placing his foot without moving anywhere. His own intentionality betrayed him. Even when he shut his eyes and ears, he could not shut off his touch or kinesthetic sense. What he really needed was a nudge, perhaps from an invisible Vamazz, to force him to step accidentally.

Since Vamazz was not conveniently present, the clockwork man broke into his most enthusiastic rendition of a piratical dance number. Almost immediately, and without any interference that I'll admit to, he stumbled, stepped between what was there and what was not . . . and fell.

And fell.

And fell.

Chalky breath puffed pastel particles at him, and floating globs of eye mucus bobbed near. Id, Ego the Maniac's younger sister, espied him from her prison and boomed primitive urges at him, demanding to know whether Ego had finishing faffing about making himself Supreme Ruler of the Universe and come to rescue her, or if she should call their eldest brother. The urges missed the clockwork man by a hair and struck a ferret-comet instead, which whizzed off after its own burning tail.

Poetry exploded and reformed in firework sparkles, if random words arranged in random patterns should, as some would have it, be termed poetry:

> Mighty fuzz
> through dies webbing
> suction
> silky markers stop electric
> toe seams

153

        and
      glorious
    whole elite
 mountains.

Skeins of baby-pink yarn crocheted themselves into light-second-long doilies that glass spiderlets clung to in hope of prey. Origami squirrels reversed and squashed their folds until rose-gold fish emerged. Butterflies played bassoons to popping balloons, inkless pens scratched pristine white dinner plates, and cactus cats suckled placid goats.

This was not magic; this was merely Pandemonisee.

PANDEMONISEE:

Also known as the Confusion Zone, the Distraction, Crazy Town, the Cosmic Asylum, and Please Don't Force Me Back There, Pandemonisee is an accretion disk spiraling around magic. Not unlike a planetary ring, Pandemonisee consists of miscellanea from across the universe that has passed into magic's pull but not as yet been swallowed by it. Pandemonisee is one of only two phenomena surrounding magic, the other being, of course, magic's satellite.

|Cross-reference, SHEEPHERDER MOON: Believed to originate when a chunk of magic got fed up with its neighbors, packed up its bags, and sprang away, Sheepherder Moon orbits whenever it feels like it and hosts the only life form native to magic's influence, the elgees.|

|Cross-reference, ELGEES: Life forms native to the Sheepherder Moon, elgees is the only species in its family. Elgees typically have

nkard, vlomistad, or dee songs. They have an
average length of 51 pearbud, including a 13 pil-
lowcase bown, weigh about 1.5–liquid, and have
a natural lifespan of blue(x-3).|

It is not uncommon for magicists who travel to
Pandemonisee to believe they have reached magic and
spend weeks or even months in the uncomfortable
location, thinking they are soaking up magic benefit.
As Pandemonisee does have a slightly magic atmosphere (approximately 205% of the concentration of
magic in Perpetua, although barely .000005289% of the
magic in pure magic), this delusion is not easily broken.
    Generally speaking, spending unnecessary time in
Pandemonisee without protective gear is contraindi-
cated for optimal physical, mental, and spiritual
health.

Vamazz the Vamazing had visited Pandemonisee on various
occasions, properly protected, to collect alchemical and sorcerous
materials that he would have otherwise had to trawl the universe for
in a much slower and less comfortable fashion. He had not mentioned this to the clockwork man, wanting his protégé to experience
it for himself. In this, the clockwork man failed, for he kept his eyes
and ears closed for the entire 13 hours, 13 minutes, 13.1313... seconds
that he fell.
    Only when the clockwork man's gyroscopic tourbillon heart
signaled to him that he had stopped moving did he open his senses.
    He saw . . . nothing.
    He heard . . . nothing.
    He felt . . . nothing.
    He imagined . . . that he was not alone.
    Power existed here, pure power strongly flavored by nothing
except itself, untainted by anyone who had come before or would

come after or was currently present. The saffron tang of Vamazz's magic was nowhere to be found. Nor was there any touch of bergamot, orange, or clove. Here was only the universal base that blended seamlessly with all of them: here was the vanilla; here was magic.

The clockwork man put one foot before the other and began walking. And as he walked, magic snuggled up close to get familiar with him. It had known he was coming sooner or later.

He let it examine him, but he kept walking. Walking seemed to be his primary task in this place: walking and discovering his new name. He did not know how long or how far he needed to walk, or if time and space were relevant factors here (though, naturally, he measured every step and every second).

Although he had accepted the necessity of a new name, the clockwork man had not grown to like the idea. He wondered if there were any way his new name could be identical to or evocative of the old one, or if this would simply be layering falsehood upon falsehood.

Between one footfall and the next, his father's shop—the Clockmaker's shop—appeared.

Time had never returned to this version of the shop. The crooked support beams like stovepipe hats supported every corner—of which there were considerably more than four. The display windows in which pocket watches, cuckoos, and grandmothers alike gleamed had had its glass scrubbed to streakless perfection. The narrow display cabinet on either side exposed the innards of clocks and the fantastic precision of the Clockmaker's craft.

No sign adorned the door; the display spoke a thousand words clearly. Besides, the Clockmaker had had as much custom as he could handle through word of mouth, in that land where time was everything.

The clockwork man opened the shop door; and here, too, everything was as he had known it: spotless edges and magnifying lenses and, on the worktable, an open watch, its cogs half out and half in, as if the Clockmaker had only stepped out for a moment.

The clockwork man stood by the empty stool and slipped on his magnification.

He knew this watch; he had seen it repaired, back before he had had hands and arms and legs to help. He had seen it after that, pulled out of his father's pocket to be wound or to be held against an ear or to be used to illustrate a concept to the clockwork boy.

The man who had been that boy looked at the watch but did not touch it, did not finish a task that had ended more than fifteen years previously.

The watch was a masterpiece, a magnificently complex piece of work, the finest pure timepiece the Clockmaker had ever made. In looking at it, the clockwork man saw what he had not before: that his skill exceeded his father's; that he could become—that he was— the greatest clockmaker who ever had lived; and that, with his imagination and Ideas, he could make such advances in clockwork as would not otherwise be gained in centuries. If he threw all his magic into sewing himself an invisibility cloak from Time, he could even move back to Perpetua and rebuild the shop. Magic would allow him that. Magic was *offering* him that.

"I am a living being," the clockwork man said aloud, "and so I grow; I must not shrink myself and return to stagnate. I am art, and so I must not waste myself by doing what others could do—or by serving Time in this small way, as my father served her all his life, save in the rebellion he granted me."

He went to the door, but emotion gripped him and turned him back to sweep his gaze over the echo of the shop. "Besides," he said, "you cannot give to me the one inducement that regression would have. Oh, why must I always lose those whom I love?"

This was not fair. He knew it was not fair a moment later; he had spoken the truth of his pain only. Yet the clockwork man's honesty was so great he could not think unfairness for long. "I have lost my father," he said, walking on, each stride as precise and rhythmic as the Clockmaker's favorite watch, "but I can visit Vamazz whenever I please, I have acquired the necessary abilities to find Puzzle Girl, and as for Raskolnikov—"

Raskolnikov! Vamazz had, in his wisdom, not permitted the clockwork man to use his magic to scry Raskolnikov's location . . . but the clockwork man no longer relied on Vamazz's magic.

Never ceasing to swing one leg before the other, the clockwork man examined magic from the perspectives of enchantment, magusry, sorcery, and spatial manipulation. In this place, he saw them as they were: not merely different ways in which to access magic, but the unique methods necessary to access individual factions of magic—for magic was by no means united. Like gravity, it had its preferences for certain beings and forms over others, and would trip up its particular favorites with mischievous glee—would allow one woman a two-story drop with no significant injury and amuse itself by spotting another's shins with mysterious bruises.

Magic, the clockwork man discovered, liked him—most specifically, those magics that reveled in a living being that had not a bit of fleshiness in him liked him.

Curious, the clockwork man brought up Vamazz's name.

The response was overwhelmingly positive. Every sort of magic vadored Vamazz. He was *vamazing.*

"What about Raskolnikov?" the clockwork man asked.

Magic did not know the name. Or did it? Perhaps on behalf of another . . .

"He is a pycckni dwarf hamster," the clockwork man supplied.

Magic acknowledged this but had no opinion; it knew him not.

Could the clockwork man contact him from inside of magic? Well, why not?

He drew lines together, in the manner of a true magus, sorting the individual threads with dexterous fingers. In the ordinary way, he would have to reach out in various directions and pluck the threads around him, to reweave. Here, magic intertwined so tightly that he had to tug out threads, changing whole patterns into new and interesting shapes. He spun the magic threads around his hands and parted them, reaching out to Raskolnikov and speaking his name.

The first part was ridiculously easy, there was so much power at hand. But when he'd reached nearly through, his fingers bumped against a wall. No, not a wall: animancy. A protective barrier, designed to keep out the uninvited. Household wards, but ones created with unusual power.

From his position inside of magic, the clockwork man could have overpowered that barrier with a twitch, but it seemed terribly unkind to destroy someone's defenses. The clockwork man therefore thoughtfully withdrew and reformed the magusry to draw Raskolnikov out instead; but again, something resisted.

This time, the clockwork man did not dare tug lest he rip his friend in half. So he released his grip and turned his attention to the foreign magic, inviting it to join him.

It followed his thread back with ready curiosity, and manifested in magic with a whistle. "Who are you?" it asked, its voice distorted by the journey. "I have not felt your magic before."

"Nor I yours," said the clockwork man. "Yet there is a familiarity about it. Perhaps you have met my mentor, Vamazz the Vamazing."

"Everyone," said the voice, "has met Vamazz. But I have heard of you, if you are the apprentice people call the Clockmaker."

"That was my name," agreed the clockwork man, "but I have no name at present, save the one I am seeking: Raskolnikov the hamster. I would speak to him."

"About what?"

"Raskolnikov," said the clockwork man, "is my friend. I have not spoken to him in years."

The voice tsked. "In that case, you're out of luck: hamsters only live for one to three years. Your friend is dead. Sorry you've wasted your time." With that, the magic withdrew, slamming the door behind it.

The clockwork man contemplated the exit indignantly. He was half tempted to swing in, shatter the defenses, and whisk Raskol-

159

nikov away.

"But there was no evil in that magic," he told himself, "and it will harm nothing to wait until after I have my name to seek him out. Only, I did wish for his advice."

On he walked, magic unfolding before him like the origami squirrel and refolding behind him into chaos that would drive insane anyone who looked at it.

"If my name must describe what I am," the clockwork man mused, "I must decide what I am—or what I wish to be. What is that?"

The answer came at once, in words not weak or faded for being well-worn:

"I am a living being, and I am art."

True, but that was not a name. So the clockwork man took the words and turned them over and examined them, combining and rearranging them and listening to their sounds even as the fluvron poets had taught him. He tried variation upon permutation upon iteration until he found one that pleased him. Then he repeated the name again and again, trying it on until it fit:

"Artilives. /Ar-TIL-i-$v\bar{e}s$/"—he had put the emphasis on the antepenultimate syllable to make it sound more namish. This did nothing to make it sound less pompous, but as the clockwork man had always—

Excuse me. As *Artilives* had always come across as somewhat pompous, and since this perception of him was not inaccurate, magic did not object to the pomposity. Vamazz might have objected to the name, not on those grounds but on the grounds that four syllables was an awful lot more than two in a combat situation, but by the time Vamazz heard the name, it would be too late to object—which is by far the best way to name yourself, your progeny, your pets, and your protagonists.

"ArTILi$v\bar{e}s$." As he spoke his name the 583rd time, it stuck in his heart of crystal and spun true. Warmth infused him from his tourbillon to his finger joints to his metal soles, his skeletonized left cheek, and his brain access panel. Magic fused itself to metal, glowing with hot brassy light and sighing a music almost but not quite completely unlike that of lyric wax, pirate shanties, and folksongs about beautiful witches and wicked maidens.

Artilives walked on mechanically, because he had been walking for so many days it would have taken more effort and brainwork to stop than to continue.

Before, he had been able to access magic—first Vamazz's, and then magic here at its source. To call his relationship with magic *access* now was to strain ridiculousness to its bounds and possibly tip it over into graveness. One did not *access* one's fingers to grip a polishing cloth. One did not *access* the ability to feel sorrow or guilt or unadulterated joy and power.

Artilives laughed; he could not help himself; he wouldn't have wanted to help himself. Brassy light shined brilliantly from his body, gleaming in every dip and turn of his engraving, racing up and down the magnifying lenses and razor nose and signed collarbone.

He could do anything, reach anywhere! Unlimited power, might, ability, agility, acuity were his! He could turn back time! Dance! Use contractions!

Harder he laughed and harder, his body jerking in time with his hilarity, his mind spiked through with such magic. Here was a being beyond any that had been seen before, a man of pure metal and magic, as foreign to the old clockwork man as the Supreme Ruler of the Universe was from a maggot fetus. He clicked his fingers in delight—

And fell hard into a clattering pile of junk, the power knocked out of him like breath.

12

The Land of the
Purple Ring

This is the land of lost things. Not the land of hearts lost when eyes meet across a crowded room, for that is only a metaphor, and is neither more nor less accurate than the one about giving your heart. Unless you are an Ucidp, no actual coronary removal and transference is going to take place.

Nor is this the land of lost time or money, unless they actively fall through the hole you kept meaning to sew up in your pocket—for things squandered or neglected are squandered or neglected, not lost.

Nor is this the land of travelers who really should have known better than to leave their maps at home but are too proud to ask for directions and therefore end up wandering off and getting eaten by avalanches. Those people belong to the gated land of Hubri City (which, to maintain its exclusivity, no longer accepts new immigrants, and never accepted anyone who hadn't a driver to do the navigating for him).

People, in fact, almost never enter the Land of the Purple Ring at all, if they're old enough not to wander away from their mothers in shopping centers and end up following around the wrong perm for twenty minutes—for one does not get into the Land of the Purple

Ring by getting lost but by being lost by someone.

This is the land of unmatched socks, eye glasses, writing utensils, wallets, keys, the last puzzle piece, drill bits, homework assignments, hairpins, and winning lottery tickets. Nearly everything here is a treasure, for it was treasured enough for the owner to miss it once gone and to have spent hours looking for it, because they were *sure* they'd left it on the kitchen table. Alas, only a small portion of the miscellanea in this land delights its prior owner in its absence; it takes real ingenuity to lose anything one desperately wishes to lose.

Artilives, with his impeccable memory and organizational skills, had in his life lost only three things to the Land of the Purple Ring: the Thirteen O'clocks, the puzzle containing Puzzle Girl's soul, and, very briefly, himself.

Dropping into the Land of the Purple Ring, he had fallen about four inches into a slush pile of unpartnered shoes and skates. A quick analysis assured him of his flawless condition. As for his magic . . .

No, he had not lost it. It no longer bashed his bones or overwhelmed the balance of his mind and spin of his heart, but it had retreated rather than vanished. He remembered snapping his fingers, all careless in magic, and was fervently grateful. No wonder named magicists did not spend more of their lives walking in magic, if that was what happened! No wonder the weaker among them never approached nearer than a glance!

Artilives felt for his magic gingerly, using a fairly forgiving type of magic—enchantment: "Wazus! Singest! Artilives!" He folded his fingers sharply toward his body, and a beeswax candle rolled up and bumped his foot.

Relieved—but interested that the candle was rather more orange than when last he had attempted this, using Vamazz's magic—Artilives picked up the candle in one hand and, with the other, very precisely snapped his fingers.

Flame flared, turning the white rope wick gold and then black in one brilliant flash, and then settled into an ordinary burn. Artilives manipulated the light and shadows, making them dance across his fingers. He coaxed the time around the candle so that its flicker first slowed to slug speed and then ate an inch of candle all at once, splattering wax everywhere.

With each spell, Artilives felt the magic clinging to him prance out, eager to be formed and directed. It came more easily to him than Vamazz's magic had—with delight in addition to duty; with love in addition to liking; with loyalty in addition to affection. Far from only springing to him when called, this magic twined about his legs and bumped his hand and sprang up when he approached. He inquired of it, and it easily gave up the truth that he had suspected: that he was, at long last, in the Land of the Purple Ring.

"Good," he said, "for I must find Puzzle Girl, and I believe that I ought to find the Thirteens. Since I lost them, days have had only twenty-four hours, and I have often heard people complain that twenty-four is not enough to accomplish everything."

Once, he would have begun where he was and gone through every junk pile in the Land of the Purple Ring hunting for the puzzle, though it took him decades to find it; now, he looked up.

No stars revealed their faces in the blue sky, and the sun . . . what a peculiar sun it was. Not the sun Artilives knew, but perhaps the sun after it had been lost, far into the future of his own time; or perhaps a star lost from far off, different in form and color and shape from the sun he knew. Who could lose a star—or what? Artilives knew not, though one day he might return to read that riddle.

In any case, Artilives knew more of divination than he could read in the stars; the clouds would serve him, if not as well, then sufficiently; and if even they failed him, he could ensorcell a piece of glass or metal or ice to serve as a scrying glass.

Glass or metal or ice wasn't necessary; the clouds responded to the divination magic he sent to them and pointed his way.

Puzzle Girl was far off, to the northwest. Not impossibly far; if the land had been smooth and stable and static, he might have run there in fifty-three hours. He might have teleported instantly, but he did not dare. He was no longer lost to himself, and therefore would surely end up anywhere save the Land of the Purple Ring, where he had striven so long to go.

Artilives encircled thumb and forefinger into a spatial telescope and peered in every direction.

Junk stretched in groaning, moldering dump heaps that belched and settled and composted hot as flatbread broilers. Former pets roved the mounds: teacup pugs and rangy cats, fat rabbits and pink-eyed mice, fierce ferrets and docile dragons, gruel-headed grosbergs and twittering tweeders.

Even if one were not 583 pounds of metal, this was not a land one could stride across; it was a land one stumbled and slid and tripped around and over, cutting one's ankles on ice-skate blades, pocket knives, and hex socket screws.

Artilives had no intention of cutting his ankles. He took these blades and knives and screws and put them together. Though he had neither forge nor furnace, he was not a mechanomancer and chronomancer for nothing. He reminded the steel that it had once been shaped, and drew heat from the heart of the heap beneath him to help. With the strength of his clockwork fingers, he bent the willing blades and reshaped the hopeful knives and kept the screws intact, because screws are always useful.

Strings of superheated metal spiderwebbed in his hands and then solidified in broad, flat circles: junk shoes instead of snow-shoes, fit for tromping over lost treasures. Each shoe was topped with a steel cage that Artilives could slip over his foot and hinge shut.

He had sunk nearly up to his waist in miscellanea by this point, and had to press and slither and shovel his way out to the edge in order to lift up each foot and slide on its new shoe.

As he had expected, progress was extremely slow. Speeding up his pace resulted in junk piles slipping and sliding away from him, burying him—once up to his neck—and sending him rolling down bumps of sewing machines and bruises of picture frames. He most-ly stayed at the valleys in between great piles, though he sometimes had to avoid a suddenly lost cast-iron single-egg pan or tent peg or lap-sized blackboard dropping from the sky.

Red movement appeared in the corner of his eye, and a bulbous head bore down on him, three times his own height. He leaned away from it and tromped backwards up a hill, but it followed curiously. A round mouth descended on him, tasting his metal casing. The words of a spell rose in Artilives's mind, and he raised his hands to pull the strings of magic, but the mouth did not envelop him or hurt him, and its gooey slipperiness did not leave behind any sticky residue. Drawn by his vibrations but blind, this was the gummy worm's only way to investigate him.

GUMMY WORM, GIANT:

One of only two species native to the blue ring of the Land of the Purple Ring (cf. LEECH, GIANT), the gummy worm is a gelatin-based life form of the corn syrup variety. Gummy worms are the second largest naturally occurring species of gelatin animal in the world, and may reach up to 200 cubits long and 13 billion calories fat.

These insatiable, affectionate, and cavity-inducing gummy worms exist in a symbiotic relationship with non-native Lotpurians. Gummy worms provide transportation and food, and Lotpurians help them shed their old skin by eating it, making the worm much more comfortable.

The worm's only natural enemy is the giant leech, which, although barely 27% longer than its prey, can slurp up a full-grown worm in under three minutes— along with any Lotpurians who fail to disembark in time.

Having no skill in therionology, Artilives could not touch the worm's mind, but the worm was familiar with beings his shape, if not his smell. When it had tasted him to its satisfaction, it lay its massive head flat in the valley and allowed him to scramble up onto its back.

There, Artilives found the rotting remains of a hide harness but no way whatsoever to steer the worm.

Feeling him settle down, the worm started off again. It wriggled around junk piles with effortless speed. Occasionally, it veered directly through a junk pile, unmindful of any inconvenience to its passenger or the way junk flew out and rearranged itself into other mounds.

Artilives clung to the gooey flesh, yelling directions that the worm ignored as it continued its instinctive route through food. Pulling and kicking the worm's thick hide did nothing to get its attention, and Artilives found himself contemplating jumping off. He would have to use magic to help him, or the landing would smash him quite thoroughly—this area of the Land of the Purple Ring was heavily metal, and the worm's speed and height would do his delicate springs and cogs no good.

What sort of magic would help him land? If only his elemental specialty were air instead of earth and electricity! He did not trust his tenuous grip of air at all. He would have to craft himself a net to land in—but how would he direct the worm to the right place? And what if it jerked unexpectedly, and he missed his aim?

The risk simply wasn't worth it. Better to be patient: the worm was a fleshy being, and eventually must slow and tire.

Even as Artilives thought this, the worm put on still greater speed, reckless speed. This was strange enough that Artilives looked back . . . and saw the leech.

Blood-red stripes streaked the navy-blue hide, thick with slime. The leech pulsated as it swam through piles and treasures. Its three-fold mouth flaps flared open, revealing triangular teeth spiraling down its throat. Sugar-lust blinded the six weak sets of eyes and propelled it forward. It made one more lurching effort and latched on to the worm's tail.

The worm whipped in sudden agony, trying to pull itself free, even if it meant ripping itself in half. Despite his grip, Artilives slammed into the nearest junk pile, a slush hole of keys.

The worm rolled, nearly crushing him, and then thrashed away again. The leech had sucked up its entire back quarter, bits of gelatinous sugar oozing out the sides of its jaws.

Artilives found himself suddenly furious at this injustice—that the worm, who had been kind to him, should meet such an end. He plunged his hands into the pile of keys and raised the land against the leech, knocking it on its side.

The leech thrashed, even as the worm had, but its sugar frenzy was stronger than its surprise, and it clung on.

That was all right: Artilives wasn't done. His hands dug deeper into the pile of keys, and they seared together under his orders, sharpening and melting into a sword, eight feet long and eight inches wide at the hilt.

Hefting it, Artilives ran up the worm's head and along its back until he came to the great leech. Then he sliced the key sword into the massive mouth, shearing away the lips. Before the leech could do more than jerk, he strode onto it, stopping on its first segment and plunging in the sword.

The leech did not die. Not because he had missed the brain—he hadn't—but because the leech had thirty-one backup brains. But the leech did rear up. It tried to release the worm, but the spiraling teeth had penetrated too deeply, and it could not free itself.

Artilives plunged in the sword once more and pulled it with him

down the length of the leech, splitting every one of the thirty-two brains and hacking until the leech lay dead. Only then did he return to the worm's tail.

In wonder, the worm was lifting itself free of the leech's split segments. The teeth had penetrated sorely, but the worm's skin was so thick and tough that it could have survived far worse injuries.

"I cannot heal you," Artilives told it, "but I can clog the bleeding."

The worm sniffed the length of the leech's body and then snuffled around Artilives again, tasting his casing affectionately and then offering its head. The sugar-blood was already clotting, Artilives saw; gummy worms regenerated at an extraordinary rate.

He patted the worm's snout, as high up as he could reach. Ten minutes later, they were on their way again—and this time the worm went where Artilives steered.

As they rode, Artilives searched out the knowledge of the Land of the Purple Ring he had gained during his time with Vamazz. Most of what he had learned was of such dubious provenance that he had dismissed it altogether, but he had gained bits and pieces here and there and where.

The only firsthand account of the Land of the Purple Ring widely available had been written by a rather brilliant academic commonly known as the Mad Don of Bullriver (Bullriver being the most prestigious university in Virulence Vale city). He wrote in a manner purposefully circuitous, this being the most accurate writing style for his subject matter, and was therefore a) dismissed by those who could not understand him; b) mimicked by those who only partially understood him, and who concluded that *purposefully circuitous* meant *obtuse*, and that his habit of precise language meant they ought to indulge in verbose sesquipedalian sententiousness; and c) studied by those who understood him and therefore knew better than to simplify and linearize his work, for to simplify or linearize it would be to make it false:

... The principle of the loss unfolds into the principles of lost, lostness, and loser. And once more it is as it has been so often

169

in the essence of the Land of the Purple Ring, that we must always hold these three principles together, must always interpret each by the other two, and yet must not bring any one to prominence in such a way that excludes or diminishes the others—neither in separating lost, lostness, and loser, nor in combining them into the false understanding. For though we may say that the loser himself achieves lostness through losing the lost simply because he experiences the loss, he is yet not the lost, and must not be called such. The loser may only be called the lost if he is himself truly lost in addition to losing—in which manner only may he become lost, loser, and lostness; yet in relation to what he has lost, he is only loser and therefore does not achieve complete lostness; nor does he become lost through what he has lost but only through himself being lost; and if he is not truly lost, then he will not enter the Land of the Purple Ring—for if all who were losers became themselves lost through their losing, then all the world, which has experienced loss, would have long entered and been swallowed by the Land of the Purple Ring, and the Land of the Purple Ring would be the world; and since our world does exist, separate from the Land of the Purple Ring, we must conclude that experiences of loss through being a loser do not equate to being lost; and therefore we must yet differentiate lost, loser, and lostness.

By combining the sparse geographical hints in *The Land of the Lost: A treatise on the nature of the Land of the Purple Ring* and folk-tales and Vamazz's vague asides, Artilives concluded that the Land of the Purple Ring's geography was one of concentric circles, the innermost of which was the purple ring, followed by blue—which was where he'd landed—and then green, yellow, orange, and finally red. Only blue, yellow, and red were populated, with the intermediary rings serving as barriers to prevent excessive mixing. And the outermost ring, the Mad Don had claimed, was the most dangerous—thus serving as a natural protection to the more vulnerable inner rings.

No one had ever reached the purple ring, that Artilives knew of.

The Mad Don had tried, but not gotten close enough to even see the sky. Each time the Mad Don had made the attempt, something different had stopped him: he'd forgotten what he was doing, suddenly remembered something urgent, stopped caring, or become terribly afraid. In the end, he'd decided this was for the best, theorizing that to enter the land's purple heart was to become truly lost to everything. Some scholars interpreted this to mean that one died, though Artilives did not.

As the worm approached the outer edge of the blue ring, the sky tinged toward green until finally, Artilives could see a clear break where one ring gave way to the next.

The border. A desert before him; treasure behind. And, if the Mad Don's experiences were anything to go by, once he went on, there was no going backwards.

"Goodbye," said Artilives to the worm, climbing down its side by using the debris stuck in its gummy skin for foot- and handholds. Only the dregs of piles remained here, scattered about, falling into the next ring: an oboe reed, a clarinet, a scattering of mink oil and cotton buds and silk wipes and tuners and foldable music stands and plastic recorders. "And thank you."

The green desert was not the green of a child's toy or even the green of grass—spring, autumn, or otherwise. Many people would not have called it green at all, but iridescent silver. Certainly, some of the individual grains of metal dust that served as sand appeared silver; but when one stared out across the shimmering expanse, across the many varied shades and tones and hues, green emerged, like the green of bog water, the green of cave water, the green of moss water, the green of deep, dark, mysterious, musty, and disease-inducing water. It might have been water, this sand, in the way it floated and shifted and made patterns at the behest of the wind.

Artilives had long since coated his casing in a scratch-resistant polymer, but he regarded the constant breezes, sudden tornados, whipping winds, high hurricanes, and other miniature wind systems over that desert with distinctly dissatisfied displeasure.

He stood, as yet, with his back to the cliff, in a nook that shielded him from all but the most impish swirls of air, considering and arranging magic. Then he held up his left-hand palm and tapped his fingers in the air. He stretched his right-hand palm down and rotated it clockwise. He shut his ears and mouth to protect them and chimed his lowest chime exactly once per second. In time to this chime, he walked forward.

Minuscule metal shards sheared at him, only to be caught by an electromagnetic field. The caught shards then acted as a shield until more shards struck them, whereupon they slid clockwise around Artilives, gaining speed until they spun off the other side of him.

In this way, Artilives crossed the green ring. He could not move at more than a march without disrupting his shield, but the desert was no wider than necessary for keeping the blue and yellow rings from merging—and Artilives's patience was wide as the ocean.

Artilives squashed into the thick vegetation of the yellow ring. Juicy mushrooms popped and squelched beneath his feet; fern fronds groped at his knees; broad, flat, fat leaves enveloped his waist. The only things growing higher were the flowers, whose narrow stems shot up from congregations of leaves to wave towering blooms at face level.

They were yellow, these flowers; every shade of yellow: lemon trifle and lemon verbena and lemon drop; mustard and horseradish and yellow pepper relish; sunshine from sunrise to sunset, with noon rays in between; banana and star fruit and egg yolk; daffodil and angel's trumpet and arrowleaf balsamroot. Yellow yellows, green yellows, gold yellows, and everything in between—yellow reigned but wasn't picky.

Below the flowers, other colors came to prominence: violet spots interrupted seafoam leaves; grizzly brown fur fuzzed ferns; maroon silk lined gray-shrouded mushrooms. Above the plant life, happy little clouds floated low, singing lullabies and sprinkling dry spots with sleepy warm milk. One cloud took it into its insubstantial mind to follow Artilives around, milking him for all it was worth and not teasing a single smile from him in return. If anything, its efforts only grumpified the clockwork man! Poor unhappy little cloud; it did not understand.

Artilives minded his steps more than he might once have, but the vegetation clustered too tightly to avoid his bruising and crushing and pureeing it, and soon seafoam and violet stained his trunk, brown fuzz clung to his shins, and mushroom goop shod his feet.

Happy little clouds are ill-suited to divination, but Artilives's memory bore him straight on, through the interbred descendants of every variety of lost plant—through the section dominated by yellow flowers, through one cluttered with coat-sand trees, through the garden of cattails and bear grass and dogsbreath smartweed, through a thick thicket of thickery—and into civilization.

Once, this had been a deposit of the universe's lost jewelry, but civilization had turned it into a town. A town of wildly diverging taste and skill. On the one hand, Artilives found houses built entirely out of earrings, artistically arranged like the shrimp in the pirate king's throne. On the other hand, he found houses constructed of necklaces, painstakingly linked but haphazardly devoid of color choice or pattern, so that gaudy silver-and-onyx skulls twined with delicate rose-gold chains, diamond-studded platinum, and plastic imitations.

Pale eyes peeped out at him from the holes that served as windows, but no one came out to greet him; and when he approached too close, the eyes disappeared and ancient voices shrieked in fright, but with no clearer words than an infant's nonsense.

Artilives walked on, and found the mushroom goop peeling off into coal dust. A wide square in the center of town had clearly once had some sort of structure in it, made of something other than gems; but now, only dust and glittering specks remained of it.

The building behind this dusty mess stood strong, its diamonds and rubies good for millennia yet. Artilives guessed it to be a public building, since it was four times larger than any other, but when he went inside it, he found only emerald shelves covered in dust and empty floors and counters. He went further back in the building, and found fragments here and there of pottery; further still, to the very back, and found half a ledger of wood and paper, and a cup of moldy coffee.

Artilives paused, struck by ancient pain and ripping fear. Then he sped into action. Ignoring the frightened shrinking of the bent old townsfolk, he searched every inch of the town, until there could be no doubt: along the edges, the buildings were pristine, with books and wooden beds and grass mattresses and even, wonder upon wonders, an infant lately lost. But through the center of town, only the gems and metals remained; all else had fallen to the ravages of Time.

She had been here, and recently. What was *she* doing here?

Artilives blinked rapidly, twice as rapidly as his tick demanded. He felt like he was malfunctioning, but a quick check revealed nothing wrong, and a more thorough search revealed the same. He polished himself from noggin to sole, but found not a scratch. His time beat true and his wheels turned steadily and his heart spun even as it should have and not with the rapid horror that coursed through it.

Time. He had not felt her presence so thickly since he had left Perpetua. How had she been lost? And what was the world doing without her?

"I am a rank two chronomancer," Artilives reminded himself. "I only have to look."

He did not want to look, but the idea that she might be close so struck him that he cycled into chronomancy and blinked twice, so he could look across the land and see every time signature.

In this stagnant place, most objects exuded only the faint after-image of time. Clocks that had kept seconds strictly for many and many a year bore ruddy outlines, however, and Artilives saw here and there bright sparks that puzzled him. He had never before encountered a lost moment.

TIME ANEMONE:

A red-spotted gray anemone, the time anemone came into existence many centuries ago, although it has not yet been recognized by the scientific community. The first anemone was born when a teenaged Time squeezed sebum out of her pores into the bathroom sink. The waxy white worm swam down the plumbing and into the sea, where it settled, grew, and multiplied.

As anemones have very little intelligence and memory, the time anemone is forever losing its crabs, fish, algae, and the moment that it could have sworn it had in its tentacle a moment earlier.

Time anemones are the only creatures in the universe that genuinely lose time, as opposed to misusing it or squandering it or, in the case of the universe, making under-the-deal tables with it. Extreme caution is advised when there is any possibility of coming into contact with one of these unique and marvelous beings. . . .

As a Perpetuan, a clockwork man, and a chronomancer, Artilives himself gleamed as brightly as any moment in time. But brighter still, though vastly more distant, bright as magnesium light—

Artilives closed his chronovision, cutting off the sight lest it burn him—for he feared that, straight on, Time's chronolight might be infinitely bright. Then he walked on, not wishing to remain in this broken place any longer, and fearing for Puzzle Girl's welfare—for her puzzle lay within a degree of Time's direction and in the same ring.

Artilives knew from the chair backs that the portion of wood holding a soul remained far hardier and more resistant to Time than its mundane counterparts; but he also knew from his experience with Sharpig's banquet table that such wood had its own, less predictable, fragility.

He did not for a moment, millisecond, or microminute think that Time's presence had anything to do with Puzzle Girl. Nor, highly though he thought of himself, had he the hubris to think that she was there for him. He concluded that she must have finally come for the Thirteens, to bring them back or to end them—or that she had come for some purpose linked to her essential nature and necessary for keeping the Land of the Purple Ring in its peculiarly static state, with the sun stuck continuously at its peak, as if it were noon—but a shrouded noon, orange and overlarge and tinting its sky the rings of a child's plastic rainbow toy, and flickering with the coolness of midnight.

Artilives sped on; and despite his aversion for it, and his native Perpetuan's suspicion of the lingering time residue, he soon took to the path Time had wrought in her destruction. Dust billowed beneath his feet and swarmed in choking clouds behind him, but he not only moved far more swiftly and efficiently than the jungle rendered possible, he also avoided mimicking Time's caustic qualities.

He came across other villages through which Time's path had wrought destruction—had not only wrought it, but had apparently veered out of her path to work, for they were by no means in a straight line. None of these villages was as large and ornamented as the first, but rather more of their villagers remained, for rather more had had the wisdom and humility to run and hide rather than emerge to gawk and gape and degenerate at Time.

They did gawk and gape at Artilives, not for his appearance—the lost were as varied a people as existed anywhere in the world, for they came from everywhere in the world—but because he sped-walked where Time had marched, headlong and seemingly suicidally after that eroding force.

The yellow jungle gave way to the orange desert. No trail of dust and charcoal and memory betrayed Time's passage here, for this desert remained in perpetual motion, flapping its fabric in mesmerizing, hypnotizing, confusticating, stultifying, maddening irrationality. The Mad Don had called it the orange desert, for consistency's sake, but inhabitants knew it as the Sock Sea.

THE SOCK SEA:

By far the most hazardous, treacherous, and foot-smelling of the Land of the Purple Ring's inner rings, the Sock Sea comprises those items most infamously lost: primarily single socks, but with keys, glasses, purple rings, wallets, nail clippers, lip balm, and other miscellanea mixed in, thrown about, and whipped through the air at concussive speed.

Unlike the land's other rings, which are content to accept lost things as they arrive, naturally and without augmentation, the orange ring actively recruits lost things, primarily by way of its only native animal (see GREMLINS).

Artilives regarded the lurching waves dubiously from the sock-littered yellow jungle shore, and ducked swiftly out of the way as a chuck key whistled at his head. This place bore more resemblance to a turbulent sea than a desert, he thought.

"I am a pirate king," he said aloud, "but I have no ship. Yet are there not legends of lost ships? One of them must surely have ended up in this place."

He got to work at once, summoning a ship. He wove magus nets and cast them into the sea to fish for ships. He called out with technomancy for any ships with advanced enough navigation systems to pick him up on their radios. He chanted the name of every lost ship from every pirate story he knew. He calculated the arithmetic probability of a ship appearing and then cooked the books up to 100%. Then he exercised his clockwork patience until the first of his ships appeared.

He recognized her. Her first owner had dubbed her the *Lady Susan* and given charge of her to his favorite captain, but she'd proven a flirtatious and capricious mistress. She'd willingly sail with any captain and any crew who would bring her glory, but she didn't care for them. Cursed, some called her, after her third crew was eaten by cannibals. Those cannibals had sailed her back to her native shores, only to find that the people there didn't take well to being eaten. Wicked, said others, after her fifth captain had been slain in his own cabin. But it was her seventh captain who had managed to lose her:

CAPTAIN'S LOG

Mon., 16th Innu.

My crew refuses to be calmed, and I can hardly blame them. I can feel this ship watching me, and I fear that after the encounter with the spirons, I have lost her favor. I know it is only time, now, before she finds some way to get rid of me and moves on to some other, ignorant and innocent captain.

I cannot allow this to happen. We are not far from port; I will send my crew ashore upon the dinghies and carry on by myself. There must be some way to lose this ship in the wide ocean, and if my life only is to be sacrificed, I would regard it well worth the loss—for in dying, I will save many other lives.

Fri., 20th Innu.

I fear she has realized something is amiss. We have now been three full days without a crew, and she has become increasingly difficult to navigate. She resists me at the wheel. I have been singing to reassure her, making up songs about an imaginary crew that we will pick up in Bertram's Pentagram—the crew of the *Maryann*.

Fri., 27th Innu.

I can bear these dreams no more. I find myself falling asleep at the wheel, and her guiding my hand. I fear that if we remain any longer, she will take me over entirely and bring us back to port.

We have seen no other ship in days, and I cannot risk any coming to our rescue. This is my last entry. I will cast myself to the sharks, rather than let her take sustenance from my soul. If anyone finds this entry, pray for me ... and burn this ship lest it swallow any other brave men and women.

Oddly enough, the captain who bravely sailed to strange waters and dove off the *Lady Susan* did not die, for he had had a selkie ancestor, and blood will out when one is stuck between a rock and a hard place, beggars can't be choosers, the sword's to the grindstone, and the pedal's to the metal. During his unconscious transformation, however, the *Lady Susan* was lost forever.

This was definitely not the sort of reputation Artilives looked for in a ship, but ships are not easy to genuinely lose, despite the jargon, and the only two ships that followed the *Lady Susan* over the cloth sea to meet Artilives were worse: the infamously ravenous *Countess Erzsébet*, whose boards were not stained by the blood in which they had bathed only because of their fanatical absorbent properties; and the *Pretty Boy*, whose rudimentary instruments were so ill-built that the ship was generally considered too impossibly stupid to take instruction. Likely, it had only arrived here, with its expression of vague confusion, because it had seen the *Lady Susan* and mistaken her for its mother.

The *Lady Susan* slid coquettishly near the ridge where Artilives waited.

"Ahoy, proud maiden!" cried Artilives. "Let down your dinghy and bear me aboard, for I am the very model of a prideful pirate king!"

A dinghy sashayed around her starboard side, sticky with a magus net. Artilives drew on the gossamer line attached to the net, pulling the dinghy his way. When it nestled snugly against the cliff, he attached the line to a handy tree, swung down, and rowed to the ship.

The *Lady Susan* preened to have a captain—and a pirate king, at that!—stride her deck in heavy boots and take her wheel with a firm hand. She strutted past the slavering *Countess* and baffled *Boy*. When her new captain, in proper piratical form, burst into a series of shanties, she practically burst with pleasure.

In this way, Artilives crossed the orange desert, the treacherous Sock Sea, safely and swiftly: in song and ship, escorted by a killer and a simpleton.

.:|:.

People lose their dangerous possessions as proficiently as, though less commonly than, their innocuous ones. They misplace rat poison and machetes, explosives and implosives and deplosives, fireworks and cigars, books full of ugly truths or pretty propaganda, plastic bags with the suffocation warnings rubbed off and creepy dolls with broken eyes that watch you sleep. They lose bayonets and corsages, incriminating documents and excriminating evidence. Voodoo dolls end up here in the red ring, along with baby teeth and fingernail clippings and brushes threaded with mats of black hair.

Artilives stood upon the shore, the song he had imprinted upon the *Lady Susan*'s deck boards dwindling in the distance. The Mad Don had written about this ring, too, couching his language in layers of metaphor to convey the feelings of danger and fear that had overwhelmed him there. Except it hadn't been metaphor.

Dark brown, green-tinged, porous rock coated the surface of the ring. Spider-web fissures split the metamorphic rock, emitting puffs of steamy hot air, heavily sulfuric and faintly mustard-colored. When Artilives looked down one, he saw the lava far below. The Mad Don had written that the whole outer ring rested upon a bed of lava. Artilives found himself irresistibly reminded of Stinking Limffort.

At the moment, however, the land seemed solid enough; and although time rested heavy in the air, it was not the frenetic time of the Mother of All Cheeses, and admitted to no inclination for swift ripening.

Unlike the rest of the Land of the Purple Ring, no treasures littered this ground; no plants grew from lost carnivorous weeds; no toxic minerals piled up in sniffable hills. The only immediate signs of life were slow-moving mounds of creatures, glowing red beneath the cracks of their rocky black shells as if they were themselves volcanic, which wasn't far from the truth. About half a dozen of these (five, to be exact) slid across the rocks nearby. Where they passed, the volcanic rock had re-re-crystalized and shone polished and clean and free of the tiniest specks of debris.

"Excuse me," Artilives said to the nearest of these, "but has Time passed through here lately?"

The formation paused, sucking at the rock beneath it. It had no speaking orifice, Artilives observed in dismay. But then, wonder upon wonders, he heard its voice in his mind—for he was a geomancer, and magmasaurs are rock-based life forms.

MAGMASAUR:

Native to the outer circuit of the Land of the Purple Ring (commonly called the Red Ring), magmasaurs are a generally benign species of scavenger. Able to envelop objects up to twice their size, magmasaurs digest by raising their internal temperatures to 2,200 degrees Fahrenheit and absorbing the minerals within their food.

Magmasaurs have no natural chromosomal deterioration and do not age in the traditional sense of the word. Instead, they grow steadily and unceasingly larger over time. The larger they grow, the more difficult it is for them to attain enough nutrition to produce a sufficiently large shell. Cracks therefore develop in their shells that predators can take advantage of. If a magmasaur manages to avoid predators, it will eventually grow so large that its shell cannot contain it.

When a magmasaur reaches this stage, it exits the Land of the Purple Ring and travels as far as it can before spilling out over the ground—which is how volcanos are formed.

"Stranger," boomed the magmasaur in Artilives's mind, "why have you come to this place?"

"To search for a friend whom I lost," said Artilives. "She is located in that direction"—he pointed—"and I would prefer to avoid Time, if I can. Do you know where Time is?"

"Time," rumbled the magmasaur, "has been cleaning up the rim. She takes the lost things that are our food and destroys them, so that we must forage for crumbs. If I had seen Time or known where she was, I would have eaten her—for we are starving, and she is the cause."

"That does not seem right," said Artilives. "Why would Time take your food? What would her motive be? She is destructive because that is her nature, but I have never known her to be malicious in this way."

"You are a strong geomancer," said the magmasaur, "and I will not argue with you. I am hungry, and must eat whatever I can find."

"Do you intend to attempt to eat me?" Artilives asked curiously.

The magmasaur resettled in ponderous thought. "Your metal content is extremely high," it said; "you would satiate me for many days. But in those days, my conscience would rebel and smite me, and I would cast myself out of this land to found a volcano. You are safe from me and mine."

"Thank you," said Artilives, who had not wished to fight the creature. He skirted its path and continued on.

After a time, he came upon a group of slaves—a collection of the most dangerous creatures in the world, from polar bears and crocodiles and hippos to flatterwats and invetrons to pterodactyls, pteroiambs, and pterospondees. Grumbling and grumpling, they trudged back and forth between a massive pile of junk that ever refilled itself and a massive fissure whose magma levels had risen within ten fathoms of the surface. With each trip, they carried lost treasures and dumped them into sloshing liquid rock below. The junk steamed and burst into flame as it fell, bounced off the surface, and then slowly settled into it, joining the magma and raising its level.

Vast heat filled the air, and red light bounced off Artilives's casing and lit the sweating muscles and miserable attitudes of the

182

slaves.

"Stop!" cried Artilives. "What are you doing? This is the mag-masaurs' food supply. You are starving them!"

A cycloptic elf rounded on him, surly and sour. "You think we aren't aware of that? We don't do this for our pleasure, you know. Who are you to judge? I don't see you working."

Artilives opened his mouth to explain, but the elf wasn't inter-ested in hearing it.

"Go away and stop distracting us," he said in disgust. "Or do you *want* Time to return and age us into dust?"

Had Time gone mad? Artilives wondered, leaving the slaves to their labor. Had she turned truly wicked instead of merely uncar-ing?

He and Vamazz had defeated many mad magicists and mon-sters. Vamazz had taught him that it was his duty to protect those he could simply *because* he could. But what could he do against Time? Surely, she could not be defeated. People needed Time, terrifying though she was. One could do nothing, without time to do it in.

"This is beyond me," he said to himself. "I must have help. Vamazz will know what to do." He raised his voice and cried: "Vamazz! Vamazz, help me! Vamazz the Vamazing, I summon you!"

Vamazz had never failed to come before. Nor did he fail to hear Artilives's call, but he had no one to lose him, and therefore no way to get to the Land of the Purple Ring, however he railed against the rules of the universe for this injustice. Artilives called and called, but Vamazz did not, could not, appear, even when Artilives used every single one of his multitudinous titles.

It is not easy to lose something you desperately want to lose.

Artilives tramped on toward the puzzle. Divination assured him it was directly ahead, not far, and he felt no surprise when his near-sighted view resolved into a hill and, at its peak, a massive for-tress constructed of the same volcanic rock as covered all the land. When he got closer still, he could see that the fortress swarmed with scowling, growling, grudging gargoyle guards.

"Who are you, and what is your business?" snarled the gargoyle posted above and to the left of the main entrance, when Artilives approached.

"My name is Artilives," he said. "I am looking for my friend, whom I lost. I have reason to believe she is somewhere inside this structure."

"A treasure hunter, eh?" said the gargoyle.

"A thief," corrected the gargoyle above the door to the right. "Time will want to interrogate him."

"I beg your pardon," said Artilives, "but I am not a thief. I wish merely to rescue my friend's soul, which Time has no claim upon or right to. You may accompany me, if you wish, to verify that I remove nothing else."

"Time has a right to and a claim on everything in this land," said the first gargoyle, "but I'll accompany you—to her throne room!"

Unhappily, Artilives admitted to himself that he would have to confront Time eventually, and that it would be better to do it before he found Puzzle Girl, for she would be safer away from the confrontation. But he was afraid, and only rigid self-control stopped him from blurring in past the gargoyles and searching the fortress from tip to toe while they raced to catch up. Instead, he waited as the left gargoyle climbed laboriously down and opened the grand front doors.

Time's taste for treasures had not lessened, Artilives saw, but her flair for the unique certainly had. Passing through the grand hallway, dark with porous stone and lit only by scattered yellow glowworms, he looked into her display cabinets and frowned in disapproval—for here were only the common things to be found in the Land of the Purple Ring: harpsichord strings and bagless bagpipes, gold brooches and silver bracelets, grizzly brown ferns in ordinary old pots and infant gummy worms.

When he had lived in Time's palace, Artilives had not known enough about the world or its possessions to recognize the rarity, the extraordinary nature of her treasures. But he knew now, and he remembered perfectly, and this wasn't right. What did Time want with a ratty safety blanket, an old-fashioned metronome, or a plaid tablecloth? These things had not been lost to time; they had merely been lost.

Artilives and his guard arrived at the throne room. The gargoyle threw open a massive door of magmasaur-polished volcanic rock, stomped within, and posed. Artilives followed, noticing that here were even more piles of junk—not displayed in cabinets or tastefully along the walls, but simply dumped in, as if collected by someone for the sake of collecting without any notion of what to do with what she collected.

"O great dictator Time!" the gargoyle proclaimed. "This intruder—"

"Slave?" the Thirteen O'clocks exclaimed in astonished delight. They swung both sets of legs off their porous black throne and hurried toward Artilives. "Slave, it *is* you!—Have our brothers and sisters lost you as you lost us?—How are they?"

"O great Time—" the gargoyle tried again. "This—"

"You're dismissed, gargoyle. Can't you see we know him?—It's our old slave!—We never thought to see anyone from our old home again. How strange!—How wonderful!—See how we've grown, slave?—Aren't you impressed?"

Artilives regarded them with nearly as much astonishment as they regarded him. Dozens of little inconsistencies from his journey clicked into their proper places, few of which pleased him.

The Thirteens were not how he remembered them, for they were of exactly equal size, but not in the half-grown state of six-thirty. Instead, both were full grown, as if it were simultaneously thirteen o'clock noon and thirteen o'clock midnight. He remembered the unnaturally shrouded sun, the twilight that belonged to neither morning nor evening, and he was disturbed.

"You have styled yourselves 'Time,'" he observed.

"What a fussy, nursemaidish thing to say!" Thirteen O'clock a.m. said.

"You're exactly how we remember you," added Thirteen p.m. "How long has it been? Nine years?"

"Nearly ten," said Artilives, "with only twenty-four hours in each day."

This correction sent the Thirteens into gales of laughter. "How

185

they must miss us!" they said. "Are our sisters and brothers very sad?—What of Day and Night?—The whole world must have mourned.—Tell us how they missed us. Was there crying in the street?—Do they wail whenever their clocks try to move to thirteen and miss?"

"Indeed, no," said Artilives. "Clocks have been redesigned to read only twelve numbers. People adapt quickly, and before many generations have passed, they will forget there ever was a thirteenth hour."

This was not an observation designed to please the Thirteens. Nor was it one that the slave they'd known could have made, for it required knowledge of the world, imagination of the future, and wisdom regarding the nature of living beings.

Artilives waited to see if the Thirteens would perceive anything beyond their own offense. To his disappointment but not surprise, they did not. They were too used to being absorbed by themselves to observe any inconsistency in others, save that which inconvenienced them.

"How could people forget us?" they cried. "Disgraceful!—Abandonment! Wretches!—As if we didn't matter!—Are we not Thirteen, highest of the numbers?—Two entire hours missing, and they *forget?*—We won't stand for it!"

"The problem is easily enough solved," said Artilives. "I will take you home."

"NO!" The Thirteens whipped at him as one, with such a fierce gust of time as would have aged Artilives a century. He caught the time subtly and clenched it in his hand, out of their view, and did not rust.

"Do you not wish to return?" he asked innocently. "I could oil your orifices and polish your noggins and tote you around to explore Time's palace."

"*We* are Time here," shot back the Thirteens. "We are queen, empress, and absolute ruler.—This is *our* palace, and these our treasures and guards and slaves. Thirteen O'clock is the only time here, and the only time there'll ever be."

Except for those time sparks, Artilives thought, heavy with resignation. He had been right, when he'd wondered if Time had gone mad. He had witnessed the signs often, when he and Vamazz had snuck into the suites of sick sorcerers, encountered evil enchanters, wrecked war upon wicked wizards, and dueled deadly diviners. He could not deny or ignore the signs, and he would not avoid his duty.

Had the Thirteens always been this way? he wondered. Every O'clock had been deeply selfish, for they had spent many hours as infants, and infants must be selfish to survive. But though some of them had been purposely cruel to him, he could not remember that the Thirteens ever had.

"I am surprised," he said, "to see you both full-grown at once."

The Thirteens twirled, admiring their bodies. "Isn't it marvelous? We fixed ourselves first thing, when we got here. It's so much more comfortable than forever growing and shrinking, aging and deaging."

"No doubt," said Artilives, "but you are Time here, and it is Time's foremost duty to maintain the flow of days and hours and minutes and seconds, rolling out fresh time each day—and by sticking yourself in this unnatural form, you have made the time here stuffy and stagnant."

"How dare you!" cried the Thirteens. "We are Time! We do what we wish!"

"Time," said Artilives, "seldom does what she wishes."

"We do *exactly* what Time does," the Thirteens snapped back. "We march as she does, destroying everything in our path—we enslave creatures and make people fear us—we collect treasures and fill our palace with them!"

"Time," said Artilives, "destroys as she marches—she does not march to destroy. She enslaves to protect and support the days and hours; she does not freeze them in place. She collects what is lost to her in order to preserve it, not out of greed or false grandiosity."

"That's enough!" cried the Thirteens.

"Time," said Artilives, "allows people to act as they will without interference. She enables their lives by promoting the natural fluctuations of her children, and if people choose to fear her—"

"Shut up, Slave!" the Thirteens screamed, and hurled a thousand years at his heart of crystal.

Artilives caught the time, and he let them witness him catch it. So strong was the swirling mass of centuries that he could see it with his naked eyes, writhing and distorting the air. "You are behind the times," he said. "I am not as I was, and you are not as you should be."

The Thirteens' eyes had rounded like sand dollars. "Impossible!" they gasped. "You should have rusted! You should be malfunctioning!—Maybe his metal is stronger than we thought. If we try again—"

"Stop," said Artilives.

The Thirteens did not stop, and Artilives saw they were working up to something enormous. With a reluctant chime, he turned on his chronomancer vision.

The Thirteens shone brightly. They shone very, very brightly. But they were not Time, and they could not blind him. He saw everything they intended.

With a hurricane's roar, the Thirteens cast two hundred thousand years directly at him.

The mass of time was enormous, far more than Artilives could safely catch or even touch. So he raised his eleven hundred years and deflected it instead. The lance of two hundred thousand years slashed away and struck the ceiling.

The ceiling could not hold it; it crumbled into nothing, and the excess time bled through the structure like lightning. Rock crumbled to gravel and rained down around them; boulders bounced off, breaking into smaller rocks, worn by wind and water and use. Greenish-black dust strangled the air and blew away into nothing.

The Thirteens screamed. They had shrunk, Artilives saw; expending so much time so quickly had deaged them. Not much— not by even a year—but enough to assure him that their resources were not unlimited.

"You've ruined our palace!" they shrieked. "That was ours, Slave! What has she done to you? How is she protecting you?"

"I am not a slave," he said. "I have not been a slave since I left Time's palace nearly ten years ago. My name is Artilives, and my

power is my own." He took the time still in his hands, and kneaded it out. Deflecting the two hundred thousand years had taken a chunk off it, but 583 years yet remained, and they would suffice.

"You can't take us back to her!" the Thirteens insisted. "We won't let you, if we have to hit you with a million years. Let's see you deflect *that*."

Artilives tossed the stretched years at them. The time grew and enveloped the Thirteens, thin and pliable as pizza dough. The Thirteens' mouths opened and their arms reached for him, but the dough constricted, and they shrank and deaged, fluctuating up and down until they settled at half-size: as if it were exactly six-thirty instead of both noon and midnight.

As they shrank, the sun sank, and night-day settled into a comfortable twilight.

As they deaged, the Thirteens also lost the sharp ugliness that had characterized their features. Their cleverness and ambition melted into childish faith, and they gazed up at Artilives with artless helplessness.

Artilives offered Thirteen a.m. his hand, which she took. "I will take you home soon," he said, "but first, we are going on a treasure hunt. We have a very special puzzle to find."

13

Onward

Time did not recognize him. She had coveted the heart of crystal, but once it had been covered up, she had seen only a clockwork slave—and she had had many slaves.

A powerful chronomancer was quite another story, and she dealt with him as her nature dictated. "You have restored my Thirteens," she said, "and it is not right that Time should be in any creature's debt. Take your pick of any treasure in my palace, and then depart."

Artilives returned the Thirteens, once again growing and shrinking apace, to their nursery. They clung to him as he tucked them in bed next to the Twelves, and he rather thought they tried to fulfill their vow of a million years. But a yawn overtook Thirteen p.m., and they subsided.

Artilives did not remain long in the palace after that; only long enough to collect a jar and enough of the Sands of Time (meticulously sifted) to fill it. Then he hurried on.

In his hometown, he purchased metal in the varieties and of the origins his father had preferred—for although he had promised Raskolnikov that he would not model Puzzle Girl on himself, metal was the material he knew best, and it must form a solid portion of her frame. The middle-aged woman who took his gold remembered him from when she'd been a girl and he but half-built. Artilives thanked her and tucked the metal along with the puzzle and the sand in a pocket of space he folded up small and stored in his gut compartment, next to his imagination and miniature repair kit.

In the Antechamber, The World's Greatest Poet and The World's Even Better Poet each wrote him a commissioned poem, and Vialia vehemently refused any payment for the music box she crafted for him, which played the music of lyric wax. She seemed alarmed by the changes in him, Artilives thought—at how powerful and knowledgeable he had become, and that he no longer used the name she had bestowed upon him. But she remained his friend, and Artilives thought she would adapt, given time.

On Artilives went, collecting materials from every corner of the world he'd visited, that had been important to him: sparkle dust from a glimmer star and golden shrimp blood from his pirate ship and the letters off a sign from the Tomb of Ego the Maniac. Vamazz presented him with a flaming sapphire-blue mushroom and asked him to investigate the Bouncing Mantis of Boolgahoo, once he had the chance. Maxwell, who had nothing else to give, gave him a kind word to remember.

After he had collected everything, Artilives turned to stars and clouds for divination, and then teleported himself outside the place where Raskolnikov resided.

To call such a place merely a tree is to belittle it beyond sense, reason, or taste. It had begun growing millennia ago and somehow forgotten to ever stop. It had grown so enormous that its inside had stretched and hollowed out, the spaces in its branches tall enough for a Perpetuan to walk unstooped. Rough bark ridges striped its exterior, and its branches had been augmented with vibrant brass cogs. Splits in the bark served as windows, and a rotating dog lever marked the circular door among the humped roots.

Artilives knocked, though he was certain the inhabitants already knew about his arrival. Sure enough, only twelve seconds elapsed before a woman opened the door.

"So it's you," she said. "Took you long enough."

She was quite a striking woman, her violet hair flowing enormously and framing a diamond-shaped face free from imperfection.

Robes draped and wrapped and swathed her in the colors of autumn leaves, and the long delicate hands ended in iron nails. Most startling, however, were her eyes: vibrant sapphire and effulgent with brilliance, for hers was a turquoise mind. Her name was Galapagos Archipelago de la Cara, and she was a wizard—but we don't talk about her.

Behind her, only pretending he hadn't run to the entranceway the instant the teleportation alarms had gone off, hunkered a pycckni dwarf hamster. He had a white belly, a brown back, and a black stripe running down his spine—and he was so excited that he jittered and spit out the Stinking Limffort stuffed in his cheek pouches.

"I am here to see Raskolnikov," Artilives said, smiling at them both. "He has promised to help."

DEBORAH J. NATELSON

A writer originally from Missoula, Montana, USA, Deborah began writing at a very young age and was soon drawn into editing. After attaining her Master of Theology from the University of St Andrews, Scotland, Deborah worked full time as a line and substantive editor until co-founding Thinklings Books, LLC, in 2019.

At present, Deborah lives in Montana once more—reading, writing, drinking tea, and playing with her Cavalier King Charles Spaniel, Flora.

You can visit Deborah or learn more about her from her website, www.DeborahJNatelson.com.

~ *Soli Deo Gloria* ~

Made in the USA
Monee, IL
07 January 2021